TRUTH OR BIMBO COLLEGE EDITION

A BIMBO TRANSFORMATION NOVEL

SADIE THATCHER

INTRODUCTION

This book is a follow-up novel to Truth or Bimbo, a Build Your Own Bimbo story I wrote with the help of readers on Patreon and Tumblr.

There were times in writing the original novel where my voters chose a different direction than I would have taken myself. I will admit, that was difficult to write at times and I was sometimes left wondering what could have been if the story was left to unfold how I would have naturally written it.

Truth or Bimbo College Edition aims to solve that conundrum. I originally set out to write a follow-up episode where I would have complete control of the outcome. However, even as I worked to guide the story how I wanted it to go, I found there were places where the story called for deviations from my original plan to make it all the more entertaining. I followed those deviations to see where they would take me.

This book was a lot of fun to write and I hope it is as much fun to read. It is possible that I may return to the Truth or Bimbo game show world in the future and put readers back in charge of the voting process. In the meantime, I hope this gives Truth or Bimbo fans something to read and enjoy.

~Sadie

I sat backstage, trying to stay calm as Philbert Regborn began the show introductions. I had watched Truth or Bimbo for over a year now. I never planned to enter myself as a possible contestant, but I needed the money.

Then again, today's show was a little different from the first season of episodes. This was the College Edition. From what I could tell, the only difference was they pulled contestants from colleges and universities instead of the general populace.

Truth or Bimbo had been a smash hit. Even though I was busy with school and other endeavors, I had not missed a single episode. I felt for Jordan, the first ever contestant on Truth or Bimbo, as she narrowly missed out on winning the game with her mind intact.

Sadly, since then, women had not fared much better. Sometimes they made it to the end, like Jordan did, only to fail on their last question. Other times they ended up missing their final question with much less money on the board.

As for my participation, I felt pretty confident. I had always viewed myself as smart. I was relatively in tune with popular culture and I had fared well on all of my history tests in school. And, to a certain degree, I felt an affinity toward Jordan. She was an expert trivia player, as she was often able to figure out the answer to a question using logic. And logic was my specialty, coming from my school work as a computer science major. Coding was like one massive experiment in logic.

I could sense that Philbert was getting close to the end of his show introductions. I knew as soon as the door to the backstage area opened, I was to walk out, smiling and waving. Both of those things were important if I had any hope of winning over the crowd. And it was the crowd that I needed to have on my side if I was going to come out of this relatively unscathed. They would be the ones choosing my fate when I answered a trivia question wrong. Not that I planned to give them too much satisfaction on that point, but I knew I would probably miss a couple questions. I doubted anyone could answer all ten questions required to win without getting a wrong answer in there somewhere.

"And let us welcome today's contestant on Truth or Bimbo College Edition, Alexis from Thatcher College."

The door opened, giving me my signal. I stood up and took a deep breath before I stepped out onto the stage. I smiled and waved to the crowd. Their cheers were amazing. I even heard a few of them chanting my school name.

"Thatcher, Thatcher, Thatcher," they chanted.

I responded by giving two thumbs up in the direction of the chants. I couldn't actually see the audience with the stage lights in my eyes, but I could hear them and that was all that mattered.

This had all been practiced, at least the walk to my seat. There had not been an audience when I practiced earlier in the day. It was important to rehearse even the simplest actions, knowing my heart would be pounding when faced with the real thing in front of a live audience.

"That is quite a reception they've given you," Philbert said as I took my seat across from him. We were seated at two consoles on a raised dais in the center of the stage. The audience formed most of a circle around us with television cameras in several areas just outside the stage light range.

"Thank you," I said, both to Philbert and to the audience in general. "Thank you, thank you, thank you."

The cheers began to die down, giving Philbert a chance to begin to interview me. Not that I noticed the fading crowd noise. My heart pounded in my chest. I could hear the pumping blood in my veins. I had to concentrate, but it was hard with my body pushing me toward panic.

"So Alexis," Philbert said, "how are you?"

Philbert had been there for my walkthrough earlier in the day. He had even told me most of the questions he planned to ask me. Asking me how I was would be top of the list.

"I'm good, Philbert," I said, trying to project a level of confidence I did not actually feel. "I'll admit, I'm a bit nervous. This is my first time being on television."

"Well, I am certain this will not be your last time," Philbert said. "Now, I understand you have something specific you are looking to win money for?"

"That's right," I said. "In addition to being a junior at Thatcher College studying computer science, I am also looking to start my own technology company. I have a program I've been creating, a platform really, that would put all of our current social media platforms to shame. I'm trying to raise seed money so I can get the business started."

"That seems like a valiant effort," Philbert said. "Now, as I understand it, seed money like that usually comes from venture capital firms and the like."

"That's normally true," I answered. "However, those firms are usually run by men and men have a hard time seeing value in woman-led startups like mine. Also, I'm trying to get this started without a cofounder, which is also a knock against me."

"Yes, I can see how you're fighting an uphill battle," Philbert said. "Well, hopefully you do well and find yourself able to answer more questions correctly than incorrectly. To make it clear for anyone watching, both in the studio and at home, Alexis will need to answer 10 questions correctly to reach the top of the money board and earn the $1 million prize. However, for each wrong answer Alexis gives tonight, she will move up the Bimbo Board and have to make a trip backstage for a change as chosen by the studio audience."

This was all information I had heard, and read, before. It was impossible to not, after signing stacks of paperwork, all to erase the legal liability of everyone involved in the show.

The rules were a little more complicated than what Philbert explained. I would indeed need to answer ten questions correctly to win the game. For each right answer, I would move up the Money Board, starting at one cent and eventually reaching the $1 million prize. Technically, I needed to only answer nine questions correctly to reach the top of the board, but there was a final question required to prove the win. It was that question that tripped up Jordan, the first contestant on the show.

"And just to highlight the different areas of Alexis' body and mind that are on the line tonight, she could face changes to her hair, face, upper body, lower body, breasts, speech, hobby and mood before she reaches the last step on the Bimbo Board, her IQ."

Philbert was literally readying the different transformation categories, going from bottom to top, just like with the Money Board as it grew from a penny up to the grand prize.

"Alexis, how do you feel knowing you could be leaving here a very different person than who you came in as?"

"I'll be honest," I said. "It's really scary. I don't know what I'll do if I get way up on the Bimbo Board. I know if I quit the game early, I forfeit all of the money I've won, but keep all the bimbo changes."

"Yes, the stakes are grave, but hopefully worth it."

"I hope so," I said. "Then again, I wouldn't be here if I didn't think I could walk away a winner."

"That's the spirit," Philbert said, leading the audience to cheer once again.

When I was backstage, I kept wanting to put off the start of the show, wishing I had more time. But now that I was out on stage, I just wanted to get started. I wanted to see what I could do. I had studied for this test and now I just wanted to take it and get it over with.

"This edition of Truth or Bimbo is a little different," Philbert continued. "Obviously we are calling it our College Edition. But we have something special today. Alexis, the producers of Truth or Bimbo and myself would like to make you an offer."

My ears perked up at this. Whatever Philbert was talking about was news to me. I had just assumed the game would operate just like all the other episodes. I wasn't expecting additional changes to the gameplay.

"One of our financial backers likes what you're trying to do," Philbert said. "While he remains anonymous, he has experience with tech startups like yours and he understands the importance of early stages of funding. He is offering to multiply your winnings tonight by 100. That means the Money Board will start at $1 and rise all the way to $100 million."

"Wow," I said, completely shocked. I could see my face in

an off camera monitor and I looked as shocked as I felt. "That is really generous."

"There is a condition, however," Philbert said. "If you agree, this anonymous donor will select your changes rather than the studio audience. That means if you answer the first question incorrectly, it will be him who decides your new hair, rather than the audience."

Oof. This was a tough one. How was I to decide? I couldn't just assume this mystery man was on the level. He might have strange fetishes that would leave me looking like a freak. Then again, he might be completely normal and actually looking to help me.

"I'll take that offer," I said emphatically. The chance to start my company with whatever $100 million turned into after taxes was better than I ever could have hoped for.

"You're sure, Alexis?" Philbert asked. It was nice of him to give me the chance to back out, but the prospect of getting $100 million for my company was too good to pass up. I need that cash.

"I'm sure."

"Very well," Philbert said. "I will say I am sorry to the studio audience for tonight's show. I know how much they enjoy voting for the contestant changes. However, this is a special offer and Alexis is willing to give up the randomness of the audience's whims to those of a man she never met. It is a bold strategy and hopefully it will pay off for her."

I hadn't thought too deeply about what it would mean to take the audience out of the equation. I had seen previous contestants try to play up the audience, getting on their good side, but sometimes even that was not enough. It meant I could focus on the questions and not playing to the crowd. I supposed I could try and play to whomever my new bene-factor was, but since I could get no response from him, I wasn't going to worry about it.

"Well, Alexis," Philbert said. "I believe it is time for me to ask you the question everyone here is waiting for you to answer. Are you ready to play Truth or Bimbo?"

I needed no time to think of my answer. "Bring it on," I said, smiling. I was ready for this.

2

The strobe lights and the suspenseful music gave me shots of adrenaline. That was going to be the hardest part of this game. It wasn't answering the trivia questions, which could clearly be difficult. The hardest part was managing my own reactions, including the sense of suspense the show runners tried to create.

But all that suspenseful music and lights meant one thing. It was time to actually play the game.

"Alexis," Philbert said, "your first question is as follows. Linux is an example of what? Is it software, an application, an operating system, or a browser?"

Philbert read the question off his monitor. The same question appeared on my console with all four options below it.

However, the moment I heard the first word of the question, I knew I was in luck. It was a computer science question. And it was an easy computer science question at that. I was certain of my answer.

"Hmm," I said as I read through the list of answers one last time. I wanted to make sure I wasn't falling for a trap. I had seen confident women in my same position choose the wrong answer, just because they rushed.

"Anything you care to say?" Philbert said.

I knew he was prompting me to explain my thinking. This, after all, was a television show and if I didn't explain myself, it could end up being a very boring episode. Not that I cared. I was on the show and they were contractually obligated to pay out my winnings at the end of the show. This might just become the last College Edition, however.

"I only wish to say that the answer is an operating system. Linux is an operating system."

"You are certain of this?" Philbert said. "If you need more time to check your answer, you can use it."

"No, I am certain. The answer is an operating system."

Philbert chuckled for a moment. "Well, let's hope your confidence is well placed. Alexis chooses an operating system as her answer."

The suspenseful music returned. It felt like my stomach suddenly jumped up into my throat. They certainly knew how to set me on edge. No amount of watching the show from home had set me up for this experience. I would need to learn how to calm my nerves on the fly if I was going to pull off the win.

"It looks like Alexis knows what she is talking about," Philbert finally said. "Linux is indeed an operating system. But for a computer science major, that is probably no surprise. Regardless, this right answer places you on the Money Board. You now have $1 when factoring in the kindness of your benefactor."

"It's a start," I said, thankful to start off with some solid momentum. If I could answer a couple more questions correctly, then I was certain I would walk away a winner.

"I assume you are ready for your next question," Philbert said.

"Like I said before: bring it on."

"Here we go with your second question of the night," Philbert said. "What musical term indicates a chord where the notes are played one after the other instead of all at the same time? Is it Arpeggio, Bridge, Crescendo, or Maggiore?"

I had really thought I was on a roll, but just like that, I knew this was not going to be a walk in the park. I might be a talented coder and software developer, but I had no musical sense whatsoever. All I knew was what sounded good. I usually couldn't even remember the names of bands.

"I take it from your silence that your familiarity with music is not as strong as your familiarity with computer operating systems?" Philbert asked.

"I honestly have no idea," I admitted. "Bridge doesn't sound right. The other three seem to be biased on Italian or some other language like that. I feel like it should be one of those."

"A valid line of thinking, I believe," Philbert admitted.

"But after that, I'm nowhere. Sure, I've raised my odds from one in four to one in three, but those still aren't great odds."

"True," Philbert said. "Is there any other option you feel you can take off the board. You could at least reduce it to 50/50."

"I'm just not that music literate. I honestly don't know which one it could be or even how I could narrow down my option choices further."

"That would mean a guess?" Philbert asked.

"I guess so." I answered. "So I'll pick Crescendo. That sounds like it could be it."

"Is that your final answer?" Philbert asked. He was giving me one last chance to back out.

"Yes, Crescendo is my final answer."

The tense music returned as everyone waited to see if I

had been correct. It was merely a guess. I knew the odds were against me. I understood the math. If only this were the Monty Hall Problem. If Philbert revealed one of the wrong answers to me, then I would have a fighting chance, but I knew I would be out of luck.

"The correct answer is..." Philbert said, taking a long pause to further draw out the suspense. "Arpeggio. I'm sorry Alexis, but it looks like you've found herself on the Bimbo Board for the first time tonight."

"I knew the odds were against me on that guess," I said. "That's the way it is."

"Yes," Philbert agreed. "The first Bimbo category is hair. Alexis how would you describe your hair currently?"

The makeup people had helped make my hair look decent, wearing it in a ponytail, but it was only through their interventions that it looked anything like it did.

"It's nondescript brown," I said. "I don't even know how to explain the color. And I don't have much volume. My hair is kind of thin and stringy, I guess."

"I think it is safe to assume it won't be like that any longer," Philbert said. "The categories tonight are Long and Blonde, Voluminous Brunette, Pretty in Pink and Hair on Fire. No, it's not luck that gave us the same categories as our first ever Truth or Bimbo show. Since this is our first ever College Edition, the producers have elected to use the same categories as our first show all night."

There were no huge surprises. I had already seen all of these options before. Jordan had Hair con Fire chosen. That gave her red hair, but there was something extra done to it that made it look like actual flames when her hair moved around her head. It was an amazing effect. I had no idea how they pulled it off.

"Normally this is where I would have over the voting to the audience, but Alexis has chosen to put the decision in the hands of her benefactor," Philbert reminded everyone. "However, before I turn things over to him, I want to hear from Alexis. If you were the benefactor, what would you choose?"

"That's a tough question," I said honestly. "I think no matter what happens, I will be getting an upgrade in the volume department. And I'm actually a little disappointed some of the brighter colors didn't make it on the list. I think the Electric Blue has been my favorite color I've seen on the show."

"That may be," Philbert said, "but Electric Blue is unfortunately not a category tonight."

"I will live with whatever my benefactor chooses for me," I finally said. "Regardless of what color I end up with, I know it will look good. The folks backstage clearly know what they're doing."

"That's the spirit," Philbert said. "And I'm sure the people responsible for your new hair will appreciate the compliment. They do great work and they do not get nearly the credit they deserve. I am going to call up to the benefactor and see what his choice is. I'm sure he will be excited."

Philbert pulled out a phone from his suit jacket pocket and placed it to his ear. This was it.

3

After giving several affirmative noises as he listened on the phone, Philbert returned the phone to his pocket. I had no idea if the phone was real or if it was just a prop. All I knew was when Philbert put it away, he seemed to have the answer to my future.

"Your benefactor wants you to know he has great plans for you, should you fail the game," Philbert said. "He has also made his decision. He has elected to go with the classic Long and Blonde."

The crowd cheered. Even though they had been taken out of the loop, no longer able to vote for my fate, they could still enjoy the process. If anything, the Long and Blonde category had been a popular one, winning more often than not when it was provided as a choice.

"Alexis," Philbert said, "how do you feel about your bene-factor's choice?"

"I think it's a classic," I said. "And I'm sure I'll come out looking great."

"Of course, that's because of the great team we have working backstage," Philbert said. "As many of you know,

Truth or Bimbo had partnered with a private company that specializes in these sorts of transformations, but wishes to remain anonymous. Either way, I know everyone here at Truth or Bimbo is fortunate to have them around."

There had been some attempts to figure out which company was behind the transformation process on Truth or Bimbo. It was rare for a company to take part in something like this without adding their name to the list of sponsors. The whole reason for getting involved was for the publicity. Then again, given the nature of the show, I had no doubt most companies wanted to stay clear. I was surprised the show had any sponsors and advertisers at all.

"Alexis here will go backstage and technicians will do their work while we go to commercial break," Philbert continued. "When we come back, Jordan will return with a whole new head of hair."

The music leading to the commercial break sounded, telling me it was time to head off stage.

I took my time, not knowing what exactly was ahead of me. The how of the transformation process was never shown or explained to me. All I knew was what I had seen as a viewer. The contestant would walk off stage and when the show returned from a commercial break, the contestant had changed.

I had little doubt that the process would take longer than a normal commercial break. Those were only a couple minutes long. But the joy of not airing the episode live meant breaks could be cut out entirely if needed. The show would be edited together for extra drama and suspense for the viewers at home.

As soon as I was off stage, I let out a sigh. It was nice being away from the audience. I hadn't realized how much their presence made me anxious. That was something to remember as the game wore on. But knowing about my anxiety could at least give me the chance to better control it.

"Welcome, Alexis," came the voice of a tall thin man wearing a lab coat. He could have been a doctor too, since they were the same outfit, but I did not get a medical doctor vibe from the man. The way he looked at me, almost leering, told me he better fit as a mad scientist than an actual medical doctor.

"Hi," I said, not sure how to respond. This part of the show had not been told to me in any detail when I was signing all those documents and contracts.

"My name is Dr. David Diamond, but most people call me Double D. I suppose with the Doctor title, it could be Triple D, but I prefer the alliteration of Double D."

Despite him holding a doctorate, his preference for being called Double D told me he definitely fit into the mad scientist category.

"If you'll just take a seat here," Dr. Diamond continued as he motioned toward a chair. It reminded me of a dentist's chair, the way it reclined. With all the wires running out the back, I had no doubt it was motorized and could leave me lying flat on my back if needed.

I followed Dr. Diamond's instructions, sitting down as he busied himself with some equipment behind me. A part of me wanted to turn and see what he was doing, but another part of me wanted nothing to do with it. I really didn't want to know how he was going to change my hair.

"This will only take a few minutes," he said as he positioned the equipment just behind my head. "Close your eyes and relax."

I took a deep breath and closed my eyes. As soon as I did, I heard a switch get flipped behind me.

At first, nothing happened. I was actually about to ask what was wrong when I felt a sudden heat build up in my scalp. A moment later I could feel my hair growing, pooling around my shoulders.

I didn't dare open my eyes. As much as I wanted to see the results, I did not want to watch my hair grow in real time. Nor was I particularly keen to see my new hair color. I didn't mind the idea of being a blonde, but I knew it would take some getting used to.

It only felt like a few minutes had passed when Dr. Diamond once again flipped the switch and the heat in my scalp dissipated. I still didn't open my eyes though. I was afraid of what I might find.

"I must say, I like the choice made by your benefactor," Dr. Diamond said. "I think you look great as a blonde. And I gave you way more volume than you had before. It was a bit sad, to be honest. But now you look fantastic."

I opened my eyes and did not immediately notice anything had changed. But as soon as I looked down and saw the long strands of blonde hair pools on my shoulders and cascading down toward my waist, I could scarcely believe it was my hair.

"Let's get you standing and in front of a mirror," Dr. Diamond said.

He helped me out of the chair and walked me over toward a mirror on the wall. I could feel the added weight of hair on my head. I knew hair was light, but when it tippled in length and more than doubled in volume, that is a significant change.

However, the moment I saw my reflection, my jaw nearly hit the floor. The woman I saw was clearly me. She had my face and my body. She was even wearing a shirt with "Thatcher College" printed on it. However, unlike the woman I had always known, I had long blonde hair. The color was as light as could be, platinum. This was a color that usually could only come out of a bottle, yet I had a feeling this was to be my natural hair color from now on.

What was more, the length was longer than anything I had ever imagined before. With the waves and light curls in the hair, it fell to the top of my ass. I was sure if I straightened it, it would fall even lower.

I had always kept my hair relatively short. I maintained a feminine style, but I had always found short hair easier to manage. Obviously I could cut my hair when the show was over, but if I kept it long, it would take a major adjustment to learn to live with it. I could only imagine all the different ways I could get it stuck, like in a doorway or in clothing, or any number of other latches and fasteners.

"What do you think?" Dr. Diamond asked. "I personally prefer blondes, but you may take the cake. I'm really interested to see how you end up. So far, your benefactor has good taste. I'll give you whatever he asks for, but I hope his tastes line up with mine. You'll be incredibly hot by the end of the night. I'm certain of it."

"It's okay, I guess," I said, answering his original questions.

I ran my fingers through my now long hair, trying to find some way that I liked to keep it. I was sure there wasn't time to put it up, not that I knew how to do such a thing with so much hair.

"Whoa," I said as a shiver went up and down my spine. "That felt, um, good."

I could see Dr. Diamond smiling behind me. It was a knowing smile. It was a satisfied smile.

"I thought you might like that," he said. "I've made your hair more sensitive. Just brushing your hair at night, will give you a small bit of pleasure. Having a man pull on it will feel good too."

"You did what?" I asked, growing angry. There had been

rumors of some extra effects added to the previous contestants. I remembered how Jordan had a thing for sucking on lollipops, or whatever else she could get her lips around, after her lips were expanded.

That was something that could happen to me too, assuming I missed another question and my benefactor chose the lips option when it came time for the face category. Getting a sense of Dr. Diamond's deviousness, I told myself I couldn't let myself get another question wrong. I needed to keep my body away from this man who had the power to shape who I was, both physically and mentally, down to my core.

"I like to give my patients little gifts," Dr. Diamond explained. "I am sure you will grow to love it. I've never heard any complaints from women after the show is over."

I didn't want to deal with this man anymore. The longer I was in his presence, the more likely I was to get violent. And I wasn't even a violent person. I had learned to control myself, despite being in a male dominated field. I was the regular recipient of sexist and misogynist comments. It was impossible not to in the world of technology and computers. I could only hope my future company would be different. Having a female cofounder would no doubt help.

"It's time to return to the stage," came the voice of a burly stagehand. To be honest, he looked more like a bouncer with a thick chest and burly biceps stretching his black t-shirt. The tattoos on both forearms told me this was a man who would not take any shit. I also knew I was no threat to him.

"Can I get a hair tie?" I asked. My question was more a general one and not directed to anyone in particular.

"I think that can be arranged," Dr. Diamond said.

He disappeared into an adjacent room for a moment and returned a moment later with a bright pink scrunchie. It wasn't really what I meant, but I wasn't going to be picky. I just wanted something to help keep my hair out of the way. I didn't want to keep pushing it out of my face or brushing it off my shoulders. Not only would touching my hair be distracting, but it would take some of my concentration away from the game. Clearly, I needed every brain cell I could spare to focus on answering the trivia questions.

I did find out that having hair down to my butt did not exactly make it easy to put up in a ponytail, but I managed. And in doing so, I only shuddered three times with pleasure. That had to be a win. Although I could feel a building pleasure between my legs. I could only hope that would fade when I returned to the stage.

"You ready now?" the stagehand asked.

"Yes, I'm ready," I answered as I stood up straight and tried to steel myself for the next round of questions. I could only hope I could find a rhythm and get out of here with minimal issues.

The stagehand led me to the door leading out onto the stage. Then with one quick shove, I found myself out in the open. The crowd cheered at my appearance.

I waved as I walked back to my seat on the dais. Philbert was there, watching me intently, smiling himself.

"Welcome back, Alexis," Philbert said as I sat down across from him. "I must say, I think blonde really suits you. What do you think?"

"It's different," I answered, telling the truth.

"Yes, I think we can all agree with that," Philbert said, eliciting another round of cheers from the audience. "The color works, but I'm sure the length will take some getting used to."

"You can say that again," I said as I sat back and found my hair getting caught between my seat back and my back. I leaned forward and managed to free my hair, letting hang over the back of my chair. Thankfully those actions did not make my arousal any worse. I decided not to tell Philbert or the audience about what Dr. Diamond did, adding a pleasure component to my new hair.

"It's time to return to our College Edition of Truth or Bimbo," Philbert announced. "Alexis, so far you are on the first rung of both the Money Board and the Bimbo Board. Due to choosing to accept the deal of one of our show bene-factors, you get more money, but put yourself at his mercy. But that means you have 100 times as much money as you would normally at this stage. Therefore, in addition to having your hair changed from the Bimbo Board, you stand at $1 on the Money Board."

"That's right," I agreed. "Now I just need to get a couple right answers and I will be on a roll."

Philbert chuckled. "Yes, indeed. I am sure I already know the answer, but I need to ask. Are you ready to keep playing Truth or Bimbo College Edition?"

"I sure am," I said, looking straight into the camera. "Let's do this."

4

"I must say it is fantastic what you are trying to do," Philbert said. "I really admire your entrepreneurial spirit."

"Thanks, Philbert. I appreciate it. I know some people feel like women shouldn't get involved in tech, like it's a man's domain, but I hope to prove all those people wrong."

"Clearly you've got a good head on your shoulders," Philbert said. "Hopefully you can keep it that way as the game progresses. Are you ready for your next question?"

"I am," I said. "I'm looking forward to it."

"Here we go then," Philbert said, turning his attention from me to his monitor. As soon as he began to read, the question appeared on my monitor as well. "What does the ROM in CD-ROM stand for? Is it Random Access Memory, Read Only Memory, Readable Optical Music, or Ralph O'Dell Menlo?"

I let out a sigh of relief. It was another computer related question and the choices were easy to decipher. Of course I could have answered this question without the help of multiple choice answers.

"That's an easy one," I said, beaming. "The answer is Read Only Memory."

"You're sure of that?" Philbert said. "I wouldn't want you to get hurt by being overly confident."

Philbert was right. Even though I knew the answer, I needed to be completely sure. I looked over the options again and knew there was only one right answer.

"It's not Random Access Memory," I said. "The acronym doesn't even work for that one. And it's not Readable Optical Music, even though music does come in CD format. And it's not Ralph O'Dell Menlo. I don't know who that is or who they are, but I'm pretty sure they're just random names that create the ROM acronym. So yes, my answer is Read Only Memory."

I looked toward Philbert and he had a pleased look on his face. I think he was telling me the importance of explaining my answers. After all, this is television and the audience can't read my mind. I have to walk them through my thinking. I filed this information away for the future, knowing I had at least eight more questions I needed to answer correctly to win.

"Very good," Philbert said. "Alexis chooses Read Only Memory as her final answer."

The suspenseful music began to play and the lights began to flash.

"The correct answer is…" Philbert said, taking his time to draw out more tension, "Read Only Memory. Alexis got it right."

The audience cheered for me, but I could tell they were disappointed. Admittedly, as a viewer, most of the fun of the game was watching how the contestants changed over the course of the game. People cared far less about getting the right answer. Still, I needed to turn this right answer into a string of them, because things could start going downhill fast if I hit a string of bad luck. If I won the money, I wanted to still be in a position to use it for its intended purpose.

"That moves you up to $10 on the Money Board," Philbert said. "Alexis, how does that make you feel?"

"It's a great start," I answered. "Getting the benefactor bonus will be a huge help if I can pull this out and win, but it's too early to declare victory. We're only three questions in, but I've already gotten a question wrong. I'll need to get a few more right answers under my belt before I start to feel like this is really doable."

"That's the right kind of attitude to have on this show," Philbert said. "And you are correct. You only have answered three questions so far. If you manage to win this, you'll need to answer at least eight more. And on that note, it's time for your next question. For those counting at home, this is number four."

I took a deep breath and tried to force out all of my distractions. Unfortunately, no matter what I did, I could still feel the tingle between my legs. As long as I had something to focus on, I knew I would be fine, but if I needed to clear my mind completely, it would push at the edge of my consciousness, distracting me.

"What color does gold leaf appear if you hold it up to the light?" Philbert asked. "Is it blue, gold, gray, or green?"

I sat there for a moment not even comprehending the question. After getting two computer questions, I had hoped I would get more of those. Computers were obviously my best subject. This was not computers, although I knew gold could play a role in some computer equipment.

Finally, after rereading the question several times on my monitor, I started to get a handle on the question. Unfortunately, this was another question where I had no idea. I had never worked with gold leaf before.

"Okay, let me think about this for a moment," I said,

trying to stall for time. "I need to apply logic to this, because I have never held gold leaf up to the light before. I didn't even know that was a thing before."

"Like other quiz game shows, Truth or Bimbo makes for a great learning opportunity," Philbert said. "While you're thinking, maybe this would be a good time to plug our new at home Truth or Bimbo game. No, you can't make your own bimbo with the at home game, but you can answer trivia questions and see who is the bigger bimbo."

I appreciated the extra time Philbert had just given me as I collected my thoughts on gold leaf.

"Alexis, care to tell us what you're thinking with this question?" Philbert asked.

"Sure," I answered. "Gold seems like a natural answer, but the question wouldn't be asked if it were gold, so I think I can ignore that. Next, blue seems too strange as a gold related color. That's out too."

"That seems reasonable," Philbert said.

I had learned over the past year that Philbert was not always to be trusted. He mainly spoke to keep the contestant talking. So if he saw something as reasonable, there was no guarantee that it actually was reasonable. It was best to just ignore him in that regard.

"So that leaves me with green and gray," I said. "To be honest, I don't associate green with gold. It's the same as blue. Therefore, I think the answer is gray. That's an easy color to have something appear."

"You're sure it's gray?" Philbert asked.

"Not entirely," I answered truthfully. "But I can't imagine it being the others. So I'm choosing gray to be my official answer."

"Very well," Philbert said. "Alexis chooses her answer as gray."

The music played and the lights strobed. I was getting used to this now.

And despite not knowing the answer to this question, I felt pretty confident with it. I was trusting my gut and my gut rarely led me astray.

"Gold leaf, when held up to the light," Philbert said, once again pausing to draw out the suspense, "appears green."

My heart sank the moment those words came out of Philbert's mouth. I had just missed another question.

"That means Alexis guessed incorrectly and she will move up a spot on the Bimbo Board," Philbert said. "Not what you were hoping for, was it?"

"Not at all, Philbert," I said. "I really thought I had narrowed down my choices properly. I guess the one positive I can take away from this is that the question wasn't a trick question. The answer wasn't gold."

"That would have been mean of our producers to give you such a question," Philbert said. "But now that you have answered incorrectly, you have reached the Face category of the Bimbo Board. Are you ready to hear the options your benefactor will be choosing from?"

"Might as well get it over with," I said. The truth was, I did not remember all of the categories from the first episode, even though I knew these options would be the same. I just remembered that Jordan had her lips inflated. They looked good on her too.

"The options for the Face category are Nothing But Lust, Cute as a Button, Wide-Eyed Surprise, and These Lips Were Made for Sucking."

The last one had been the one Jordan had ended up with. Admittedly, when all was said and done, her lips looked great, but they were definitely the lips of a bimbo and not of a normal woman.

"Any of those strike your fancy?" Philbert asked. "I know you don't get a choice, but you must have an opinion."

"I really don't know," I answered. "I've seen them all in some fashion in past episodes, but I can't imagine them on my face. I wouldn't even recognize myself anymore, especially after the change to my hair."

"I can imagine how hard this is for you," Philbert said. "As we wait for your benefactor to contact me, I must say that you have been quite lucky thus far. Usually our producers don't give contestants so many questions in their wheelhouse, so to speak. You've gotten two computer questions already. What do you think about that?"

"Hmm," I said, considering Philbert's words. "I hadn't given it too much thought, obviously. I've been focusing on the game. But you're right. They have been giving me a couple easy questions. I'm not sure why. Maybe they're trying to even out the average difficulty of the questions. That doesn't bode well for me though. If they keep throwing my softballs, that could mean their other questions are significantly harder."

"Definitely things to consider," Philbert said just before his phone started to ring in his pocket. "But it sounds like your benefactor is ready with his decision."

Philbert pulled the phone from his inside jacket pocket and placed it to his ear. He said nothing as he simply listened. His eyes seemed to flit back and forth between his monitor and me.

For whatever reason, this call seemed to take longer than the first. I wondered if they would edit part of the call out, shortening the span to make for better television. Probably. I wasn't sure if I wanted to watch my own episode when it finally aired. Either way, when Philbert hung up the phone, I knew I would find out my fate.

5

"Sorry about the length of that call," Philbert apologized as he returned the phone to his pocket. "We had a three-way conversation to include one of the producers. It seems your benefactor has a deal he wants to offer you. He will move you up an extra level on the Money Board if you accept all four facial options. It seems he just can't decide which one he likes best."

"Oh my," I said, overwhelmed by the offer. Getting a leg up now on the Bimbo Board would be big. The question was whether I could manage to live with all four facial changes. There wasn't a whole lot of overlap in them. It was just the Nothing but Lust and Wide-Eyed Surprise that could cause some issues. The real question was whether I could handle looking like a sex-crazed bimbo, even if I wasn't one. Would people be able to take me seriously?

"I realize this is a lot to decide all at once," Philbert said. "Unfortunately, we don't have a lot of time to decide. We need to get moving with the next part of the show."

"I'll do it," I blurted out. I didn't know why I said it. I was only going from $10 to $100. That was such a tiny amount.

However, I knew it would make it easier to reach the top of the Money Board and win the game. This meant I would be one step closer to the $100 million prize.

Philbert smiled. "Hopefully you don't come to regret your decision." He turned toward the audience and the camera. "We'll now send Alexis off to have her face reworked. When she returns after our break, we will see a whole new woman."

I walked left the stage, unhappy. This experience was not going as I had hoped it would. It was nice that they were giving me easy computer questions, but taken as a whole, I didn't like where things were headed. And I didn't exactly feel good about accepting my benefactor's proposal of moving up the Money Board to get all four facial changes.

It was worse, because I didn't even know how I could look surprised and lustful at the same time. I was sure Dr. Diamond had a plan though. And I was pretty certain I wouldn't like that plan either.

"Welcome back, my dear," Dr. Diamond said in greeting. "I must say, I like your attitude in choosing your benefactor's offer. He has given me a challenge, but I am certain I will find a solution. I always do. That's why I'm here. Usually I'm interpreting the desires of the audience, but now I get to please just one man. It's a nice change of pace."

"Fine," I said as I threw myself down into the chair. It seemed obvious that he would have me sit again. The less interaction I had with him, the better. He already creeped me out. Now he was in a position to completely change my life. I understood what I had signed up for, but I still wasn't happy with it.

In fact, I was beginning to regret taking the offer. Yes, moving up a spot on the Bimbo Board would be good for my overall chances, but it still meant changing my face forever. For all I knew, I would come out of this completely unrecognizable. That didn't sit well with me.

"Just close your eyes and this will all be over soon enough," Dr. Diamond prompted.

I did as he suggested. I didn't want to watch him work. There had been a big part of me that had been fascinated in the transformation process, but that had been when I was a viewer. Now that I was actually sitting in the chair, I wanted nothing to do with this strange and unbelievable technology.

I could scarcely believe my own thoughts, given how important technology was to me, but it had never been more clear the power tech companies had over people. There was a certain amount of hubris in what they did. I needed to watch for that in my own company once I finished on the show. Then I could drop out and join the ranks of the tech billionaires. I was certain that was part of my future.

Dr. Diamond spent several moments fiddling with equipment. I could hear him practically hovering over me. When the machines behind the chair began to hum, I knew it had started. A moment later and I could feel a tingling sensation building in my face.

I wanted nothing more than to run away, but I didn't dare move. There was no way I was going to screw up whatever Dr. Diamond had started. I didn't want to look disfigured for the rest of my life. I was afraid that was just what would happen if I tried to run.

Not that the stagehands would let me run if I tried. I had little doubt they would chase me down and catch me before strapping me down to the chair to finish the process. I had signed the paperwork, making this all legal, but I also realized why the stagehands looked more like bouncers than people who worked in the television industry. They were muscle to keep me in line.

I felt like I sat in the chair with my face tingling for a long time. My sense of time was off. That was often the case either when I was mad or when I was excited. In this case, it was the former. I was unhappy and mad with myself for letting myself fall into this position. I should have been more careful. I should have rejected the offer that would forever more make me look like a complete bimbo.

"And I'm done," Dr. Diamond announced as soon as the tingling finished. "Whew, that was tough. I think that had been the most difficult facial work I had done on this show. Then again, that's what happens when trying to combine four different options. Oddly, the only ties we've had have been in psychological categories."

That reminded me of another fact. Every time I moved up the Bimbo Board, I would get closer to those psychological categories. Not only would those change my mind, but they could also make finishing the game more difficult.

I remembered watching one episode where the Speech category left the woman constantly lying. She could not give the right answer the rest of the game, since she always had to lie. And they finished the game out with easy questions too, ones that everyone should know. She clearly did, because she gave the wrong answer for each and every question remaining. It was a strange end to the episode, but she kept the series going without a winner.

In fact, in the year since the show started, the first contestant, Jordan, had come the closest to winning. It came down to the final question. She had answered nine questions correctly. She had earned the $1 million. But she needed to prove it to win and she failed. She is apparently popular on the strip club trivia circuit at least.

"Let's get you up so you can see the new you," Dr. Diamond said.

I refused his helping hand and pushed myself to my feet on my own. I then walked over to the mirror, the same one where I first saw my blonde hair.

"You've got to be kidding me," I said as I looked at my

new face. My nose was smaller and narrower. It was slightly turned up at the end. Overall, it was perfect, almost doll-like. This was the kind of nose that women would pay surgeons thousands of dollars for and pray the surgeon had the necessary skill to pull it off. Few actually did.

But as shocking as my new nose was, so too were my lips. They were thick and juicy. I just wanted to lick them. I stuck my tongue out and explored the new expanse of flesh. My eyes widened in surprise as another shudder of pleasure shot down my spine.

"Are you trying to turn me into a freak?" I cried. "My lips are too sensitive."

"I think you'll come to enjoy that sensitivity," Dr. Diamond answered calmly. "Everyone else has. Then again, everyone else seemed to be too preoccupied sucking cock whenever they get the chance. I'm sure you'll join them eventually."

I turned to stare at Dr. Diamond. I wanted to glare at him to show him my displeasure. However, instead of glaring, I found my gaze softening. My eyelids dropped as I licked my lips, sending another shudder down my spine. I couldn't help it. Looking at him put me into this weird lust mode.

I turned back toward the mirror and watched as my lustful expression disappeared and became replaced with wide eyes and a surprised expression.

"I think you're starting to understand, but let me explain," Dr. Diamond said as he came up behind me. The moment he appeared in the mirror reflection, my expression grew lustful once again. "Your default expression is to be surprised. The raised eyebrows and wide eyes will be your normal. That is, except when you are looking at someone. No matter who they are, you will get the hooded eyes and lustful stare, even adding in some lip licking for good measure. Basically, everyone will assume you're a sex-crazed idiot. You'll either look dumb or like you want to jump someone for a bout of rough sex."

I wanted to be mad. I was more than pissed off. I clenched my fists in rage, but my face didn't show that. It only showed lust as I licked my lips for a third time.

"God damn it," I cursed as I turned around, ready to hit Dr. Diamond in the face.

I even got as far as bringing my arm back, ready to strike, but then a big strong hand wrapped around my wrist. It wasn't Dr. Diamond. He was actually stepping back, cowering in fear, realizing he had not seen the rage building inside of me.

The hand holding me back was one of the burly stagehands. He towered over me, staring me down. I don't know how he knew what I was about to do, but it told me he had experience as a bouncer. Reading people like that was a skill they developed.

"It's time to go back on stage," the stagehand said.

I didn't want to go out there. After what Dr. Diamond had done to me, I wanted nothing but to return to the green room and curl up on the couch there. Unfortunately, that wasn't going to be an option.

"Can I have a moment?" I asked. Luckily, my tone of voice did not match up with the lust that was practically painted on my face. I had no idea how I was going to manage a business of my own like this. I couldn't look like I was coming on to every person I worked with.

"30 seconds," the stagehand said.

I closed my eyes and took a deep breath, trying to calm myself down. It didn't help that those pleasurable shuddered from licking my lips had added to my arousal. How did all those women who came before me handle this? Dr. Diamond was a complete monster for these little tricks. First it was the hair. Now it was my lips. How else would he screw with me before this night was through?

"Okay, I'm ready," I finally said, making it a point not to make eye contact with the stagehand. I was already trying to decide how to best play things out on stage. If I didn't focus on any one person, I might be able to avoid the lustful expression that came so naturally. That also might mean I could avoid licking my lips and making my arousal even worse.

As I stepped out on stage again, I smiled and waved. The crowd whooped and hollered as I made my way to my seat. I was thankful the stage lights prevented me from seeing the audience members. I would just need to avoid looking at Philbert and I would be fine.

"Welcome back, Alexis," Philbert said, greeting me. I made it a point to look past his shoulder, trying to keep my focus off of his face. "My, you certainly have a new look. I can see your nose and lips have changed. And the wide eyes certainly leave you looking surprised. But as I recall, there were four options. Where is that lustful look?"

I didn't want to do it, but I knew I had no choice. I lowered my gaze and looked Philbert right in the eyes. I could feel my expression change without me even trying.

"Wow," Philbert said. "That lustful look really brings the heat."

The audience sent out another round of cheers as Philbert mocked fanning himself with his hand. I felt my tongue want to creep out and lick my lips, but I managed to keep my lips shut. However, that only seemed to force me to make a kissy face, as if I wanted to kiss Philbert. As the man was at least three times my age, if not more, that was definitely not something I wanted to do.

I looked down and focused on my monitor. I could feel my face return to its natural surprised look. Some women had resting bitch face. I now had resting surprised face. It was going to be an interesting future. I only hoped I could find some measure of control after all this was over. That, or I would use some of my winnings to pay Dr. Diamond, or someone else, to fix my face.

"I must say," Philbert continued. "Our technicians back-stage certainly showed off their skills with your new face, Alexis. How does it all feel?"

"I can't say I'm a big fan," I answered. "I can't really control my facial expressions right now."

"I'm sure you will develop some control in the future," Philbert said. "That is assuming you are able to win the game."

I didn't want to think what losing would mean now. The final lowering of my IQ would leave me with almost no willpower of my own. I might not be able to control my facial expressions. Then again, I might not want to. I either would be surprised and confused or incredibly horny. I might not be capable of other emotions.

"And speaking of the game," Philbert said. "We should remind everyone that with the offer Alexis accepted before we left you, she gets to move an extra spot up the Money Board."

He motioned toward the two boards. The Bimbo Board had the bottom two categories lit up. The Money Board featured three levels lit. I might not like my new face, because of its quirks, but I had to admit I looked cute and I now only had to answer seven more questions correctly to win the game. It wasn't all bad.

"I have to keep reminding myself what I got out of that deal," I said, speaking toward the camera and purposely not looking at Philbert. I needed to make that a habit going forward. Only look at people when I absolutely needed to.

"Yes," Philbert said. "I think everyone could be considered

a winner with that one. But now the question must be asked. Are you ready to continue playing Truth or Bimbo College Edition?"

I needed no time to think of my answer. I wouldn't have taken the benefactor's offer if I intended to quit. And now that I had found myself with facial expressions I couldn't completely control, I knew I was in this for the long haul. No matter what happened, I would see this through to the end.

"I'm ready," I answered decisively.

"I must say," Philbert said. "When they first suggested a College Edition of the show, I had my doubts. We've actually had some college-aged contestants on the show before, but this is obviously a bit different. And I must say, you, the producers, and your benefactor have not disappointed in the slightest. This very well may be our best show ever. And I say that with us less than halfway in."

I had to agree that Philbert was right. Even though I disliked what had been done to me thus far, it would make for good television. If only I weren't the woman sitting in my chair. Then it would be perfect for me too.

"I'm glad I can help," I said, feeling the need to keep myself involved in the conversation.

"Unfortunately I will not be able to help you with your next question," Philbert said. "Are you ready to hear it?"

"Yes," I said, keeping my eyes focused on the monitor in front of me.

"Here we go," Philbert said before the monitors showed the question. "Which is not a computer language? Is it BASIC, C++, LOTUS, or JAVA?"

I couldn't believe what I was seeing. It was another easy question. I actually knew, at least parts, of all three of the real languages listed.

"This is too easy," I said, unable to hold my tongue. "I know BASIC, C++ and JAVA. Or at least I know enough to code a few basic things in each. I'm solid on JAVA though."

"That's impressive," Philbert agreed. "What is your answer then?"

"My answer is LOTUS," I said. "That's not a computer language. It's a flowering plant and a kind of sports car."

"Impressive," Philbert said. "Do you need a moment to reconsider?"

"No, I'm certain. The answer is LOTUS."

After the trials that resulted from the last question, it was nice to have an easy one in there. It gave me hope that I could win some real money this game.

"Alexis chooses LOTUS," Philbert announced.

The music began to play, but it had no effect on my heart rate or adrenaline levels this time. I was that confident.

"And Alexis is right," Philbert said. He didn't even bother to hold for suspense.

The crowd cheered for me, but it felt halfhearted. I didn't blame them. After what happened with my previous question, they wanted more carnage. Thankfully, I was in a position to withhold that from them, at least for now.

"With that right answer," Philbert continued, "Alexis moves up on the Money Board. She now had $1,000 in the bank. Tell me, Alexis, it must feel good to now be two rungs higher on the Money Board than the Bimbo Board."

"It does feel good," I answered. "But I'm not jumping for joy yet. I still need to get six more questions right to win the game. But even if I trade questions from here on out, I will still win. That does feel good."

"I bet it does," Philbert said. "And while I want you to be

able to enjoy your success for a moment, we do need to continue the game. Are you ready for your next question?"

"Bring it on," I shouted, trying to pump up the crowd. They cheered much more enthusiastically this time. I wondered if they were thinking they might see the first winner on Truth or Bimbo. I know I was beginning to wonder that.

Philbert chuckled as the cheers died down. "Here we go for your sixth question. What is the family name of the ruling dynasty of Monaco? Is it Amsberg, Bourbon, Grimaldi, or Windsor."

After getting an easy computer question, I was once again faced with a random question I couldn't begin to know. Ruling dynasty? I didn't even know there was a ruler in Monaco, at least not a royal figure. I thought most of those monarchs were gone.

"Hmm," I said, realizing I needed to say something for the audience to follow along with my thoughts. "I'll be honest. I didn't even know there was a ruling dynasty of Monaco. The only name I recognize on that list is Windsor, but I only know that because it's the British Royal Family name."

"Understandable," Philbert said. "What do you think of the other names?"

"I'm not sure. As I recall, Monaco is on the southern coast of France. I suppose that means the family name would sound French, but I don't actually know."

"I can see how that could be assumed," Philbert agreed.

"Grimaldi sounds Italian and Amsberg sounds German," I said. "I didn't know Germany had any royalty, but what do I know? That leads me to think the answer is Bourbon. I guess it is more than just a kind of alcohol."

Philbert chuckled at my comment. "Are you sure? Do you want to reconsider?"

"No, I think I'm good," I answered. "I'm going to choose Bourbon as my answer."

"Alexis chooses Bourbon as her answer," Philbert announced. The music came on and the lights flickered and flashed before the camera switched to a close up of our faces, using split screen to show our reactions. "The correct answer is… Grimaldi."

"Ugh," I said as I realized I had answered incorrectly.

"Unfortunately for Alexis," Philbert said, "that answer will move her up a spot on the Bimbo Board. The next category is Upper Body. But before we get to that, I do want to bring Alexis' attention to some geography and history, not that it may matter in the end if she becomes a bimbo."

The audience laughed at Philbert's joke. I wasn't very happy about being made fun of for a wrong answer, but I was interested in hearing the truth.

"Grimaldi is the ruling family of Monaco, a principality near Nice, France and also near the Italian border. Grace Kelly, the actress from the 1950s married into the Grimaldi family and was the mother of the current Prince Albert. Further, Bourbon was the French royal name, but they married into the Spanish royal family. Spain still has a monarch, France does not. And for Amsberg, they aren't German per se. They are Dutch."

"Well, that goes to show you how little I know about European history," I said, trying to make light of how poorly I did with that question. "I'll probably need to study that more if my company ever makes the move into the European Union." I still had hopes that I would use my winnings as seed money for my tech company. However, with each missed question, I couldn't help but feel that my chances were dwindling quickly.

"Probably a smart thing to do," Philbert said. "Take this as a learning moment. However, we must return our attention back to the game. It is time to give your upper body a makeover. The options are Wafer Thin, Partial Hour Glass, Strong-Armed Lady, and More to Love."

I was pretty sure I knew what would be chosen. It was almost always chosen. Partial Hour Glass matched up perfectly with the Lower Body category look. It meant a thin waist and a normal chest and shoulder size. That ignored the breasts which were a different category. But over the past year, the other options had been selected, among others that were not included in tonight's game. Some led to comical results, others what one would expect.

"Before I take the call from your benefactor," Philbert said, "I feel I should ask you what you would prefer."

"I know Partial Hour Glass is the popular one here," I said. "And to be honest, I think it looks the best. If I had to choose between the others, I guess Wafer Thin would be my preference. I don't need lots of muscle to lead a tech company and I'd prefer not to be overweight. You might not know it from looking at me, but I have worked hard to avoid putting on weight in college."

It was impossible not to add a few pounds with all the food in the dining halls and my penchant for sitting at my computer most of the time, but in the last year in particular, I had made it a point to watch what I eat. I even cut soda from my diet, which was a major achievement. Nor guzzling down all that sugar everyday was a big help.

"Well, we will find out in a moment," Philbert said as his phone began to ring. He pulled it from his pocket and put it to his ear. Then I was left waiting to learn my fate.

7

The call did not last nearly as long this time. Philbert lowered the phone from his ear and returned it to his inner jacket pocket. Then he looked toward me.

For a moment I forgot that I was trying not to look at Philbert. All of a sudden I could feel my face shift and my tongue come out and lick my lips.

It was the shudder of pleasure that shot down my spine that made me look away. I felt shame for looking like I was coming onto the show host. And I knew everyone was watching me. I was certain that would make it into the show.

"That was a simpler call," Philbert explained, ignoring my facial expressions. "But he was very emphatic about what he wanted. Are you ready to hear his selection?"

I kept my head down as I answered meekly, "Yes."

"Audience, are you ready to hear the benefactor's selection?" Philbert asked.

The audience was much more forceful in their answer. They gave a resounding "Yes," followed by cheers and possibly even a marriage proposal. I couldn't be sure. I could only assume he meant me.

"All right," Philbert said. "This is the benefactor's selection. And it is little surprise that he has selected Partial Hour Glass."

A wave of relief flowed over me. The good news, overall, was my benefactor seemed to have fairly normal tastes, at least as far as bimbos were concerned. I could only hope a similar choice was made, should I fail another question.

There had been quite a debate online about Truth or Bimbo and the proper strategy to make sure the contestant did not finish the game looking especially strange with the Upper and Lower Body categories. Some people advocated for intentionally missing a question to make sure both physical transformations were completed.

Not that it mattered, however. No one had one the game. Jordan remained the best ever and she still ended up as a complete bimbo. At least she also won the full monetary prize. That money went toward funding her new lifestyle and needs. It's expensive to be a bimbo.

"I have to say that is a bit of a relief," I said. "That has always been my preferred result for the Upper Body category."

"Completely understandable," Philbert said. "And with your next transformation decided upon, it is time to send you off to have it done. When we see you next, you will again appear a little different from the woman we have before us now."

"Thanks," I said. "I'll be back soon enough."

The music played me off the stage and the crowd cheered for me.

"Welcome back, Alexis," Dr. Diamond said as soon as I stepped backstage. "I'm glad to see you again."

I made the mistake of looking at his face and felt my face relax as I licked my lips seductively.

"I hate you," I said, in contradiction to my expression. "And you come across as a complete creep."

Dr. Diamond shrugged his shoulders. "What do you expect from a man who has made it his life's work to help women get in touch with their real selves?"

I just shook my head and turned away from the man who controlled my transformation process. As I did so, I could feel my face return to its stock position of surprise and confusion. I vaguely wondered if I could retrain my face to appear differently, maybe through an acting class or something. The natural tendencies of my face needed to be overcome so I could appear as a normal person again.

"Where do you want me?" I asked, realizing that the chair may not be the best place for me as he reshaped my torso.

I had to admit it would be nice to lose some of the fat around my belly that had built up over the years. I didn't get nearly enough exercise, even though I did try to eat healthy. My sedentary lifestyle had its drawbacks.

"Let's have you stand over here by the wall," Dr. Diamond motioned.

There was an open space on the far side of the workshop. An X marked in tape indicated where I needed to stand.

"And I'm afraid I'm going to need you to remove your top for this," Dr. Diamond continued. "I can't have clothing blocking my view."

I hesitated for a moment as I took my place. I did not want to stand before this creep of a man topless. It went against everything I believed. However, I also realized mine were not the first set of breasts he would have seen. He had seen every contestant's breasts since the show started.

"Fine," I finally said as I pulled my top over my head.

"Don't worry," Dr. Diamond said. "After this I'll have wardrobe bring you a new top. We need your clothes to fit perfectly. That's something we learned after our first show."

I remembered watching how Jordan kept altering her clothing to better fit her new body. That first episode had kept her wearing the same clothes after every round and it became clear that she needed other styles to fit her changing body. Since then, the contestant's regularly changed after significant transformations, allowing the audience to better see what they had voted for.

I tossed my top onto the floor nearby. It seemed I wouldn't need it anymore. That was fine by me. Even though it had Thatcher College printed on it, it wasn't actually my top. The show's wardrobe department had given it to me to wear. In fact, my whole outfit had been chosen by them, including the shoes on my feet.

"Just stand still and this will be over in a moment," Dr. Diamond said as he positioned a machine that looked similar to an x-ray machine. He took his time lining everything up correctly, even double checking the distance between the machine and my body.

"And here we go," Dr. Diamond said as he flipped a switch. My body became bathed in a warm red light, although its primary focus was on my torso and arms.

I closed my eyes as I stood there as still as I could manage. I didn't want to look at this man who called himself a doctor. I just wanted this ordeal to be over. I could quit anytime, but I knew the consequences of doing that. It meant I kept the physical changes to my body and I would lose all the money I had won so far. $1,000 may not seem like a lot, but I knew of several good uses I could put it toward.

However, I was nowhere near my quitting point. With each question I answered correctly, I would move up the Money Board, adding a zero to the end of the previous amount with each step. I only needed to answer two more questions to reach the $1 million level. But even that was not enough for my goals. I needed the full $100 million on offer to give me the peace of mind as I created my own tech company.

"And we're all done," Dr. Diamond suddenly said. He flipped off the machine and the warm light turned off with it.

I looked down at my naked torso. My waist was tiny compared to only a few minutes ago. I vaguely wondered how many inches my waist was now. It couldn't have been much more than 20 inches, if that.

"Wow," I said, staring down at my waist. It didn't seem possible, but I was staring at it with my own eyes.

"Quite impressive, if I do say so," Dr. Diamond said. "Hopefully you appreciate your arms as well. I've removed quite a bit of the extraneous body mass to give you your new shape. I hope you appreciate it."

Oddly, I did. Without even thinking about the fact I was topless, I wandered over to the mirror to get a better look at myself. I looked absolutely fantastic, although my normal legs, hips, and butt meant I looked a bit strange, but it was nothing to be overly worried about. Given my luck thus far, the odds were I would be returning to have my legs and ass altered.

"What did you do to tease me this time?" I asked. I couldn't sense there was anything additional turning me on. That seemed to be something Dr. Diamond liked to do. He liked to find ways to increase my arousal to distract me and make it more likely I would return.

"Me?" Dr. Diamond asked with mock innocence. "I haven't done anything to you except what you can see. Talk about a lack of gratitude. I bet you haven't had a waist this thin since you were a little girl."

I had to admit that was true. Maybe Dr. Diamond wasn't the creep I had made him out to be. Yes, he had given me a few add-ons, but I had never looked this good before. I might even come to enjoy what had been done to me thus far.

"I'm sorry," I said, bowing my head in shame. "I didn't mean to accuse you of anything. I just assumed you were playing a trick on me."

"Why would anyone want to play a trick on you?" Dr. Diamond asked. "You're cute and sexy. Everyone will want to be with you."

Even though I wasn't watching Dr. Diamond directly, I could sense that he was once again being a creep. The way he said that everyone will want to be with me told me what he really thought. Everyone will want to fuck me. I had no plans to let that happen until I was solidly in control of my new company, and maybe even after we had gone public.

"Can I get a top now?" I asked. "I need to go back out on stage."

Dr. Diamond looked disappointed in my haste to return to the game, but even he had to understand that there was going to be nothing that happened between us. I might like the small-waisted look on me, but I wasn't going to do anything sexual with the man who had otherwise traumatized my life.

Pressing a button on what looked like an intercom panel, Dr. Diamond spoke, "Our contestant is ready for her new game uniform."

A moment later another man entered the workshop area. My first thought was to wonder if all the people involved in the show were men. As I stood there thinking about it, I couldn't remember a single woman on the staff. That should have been a red flag, but I hadn't been paying attention before.

"Here you go," the man said, holding out a pink tank top. "Do you need help putting it on?"

"No, I think I can manage," I said as I took the offered top from his hands.

I held up the top to get a good look at it before I slipped it over my head. Like my original top, this one had the words Thatcher College printed on it.

I pulled the tank top on over my head. Pulling my long ponytail through proved to be a slightly erotic experience. My body visibly shook and shuddered as a strong wave of arousal flowed down my spine from my head to my pussy.

For a moment, I considered asking to use the bathroom, simply so I could have a place to find some relief to my arousal. However, I knew there wasn't time and I did not want to get found out for masturbating. That seemed like a sure fire way to get into trouble. And the delays might get me kicked off the show.

It took me a moment to arrange the top on my torso. It was shorter than my previous top, leaving a belt of toned flesh visible around my midriff. It was also a bit lower cut than what I would have normally worn. It showed off the cleavage I never really had.

In fact, my near non-existent cleavage was even more on display, considering the loss in weight on my torso had results in my breasts shrinking as well. I hadn't considered that fact before. It left me looking even more bottom heavy than I had imagined I would have.

"Time to go back out on stage," the burly stagehand said.

I looked up into his eyes, looking for some sort of emotion from him. He seemed a very stoic man. That made for a good bouncer, but it made it difficult to know what he was thinking. All I could sense, if I could sense anything about him at all, was how showered the barest flicker of attraction toward me.

Given his size, I could only assume he could stretch his big meaty paws around my waist, fully enclosing it without a gap. And if his hands were so big, I could only imagine what other parts of him were big.

"I'm coming," I said as I hurried toward the stagehand waiting at the door.

I didn't dare look at him as I passed him. I knew I would end up looking on at him with a lustful stare. I didn't need to give more men the idea that I was interested in them. I was straight, but I wasn't easy and I believed it was a man's job to chase after a woman, as opposed to the other way around.

The moment I walked out on stage, the crowd erupted in a loud round of applause and cheering. I waved and smiled, looking more and more like a bimbo. It didn't help how I felt more aroused than ever after having to arrange my hair after putting on the top. I also knew there was nothing I would be able to do about it until after the show. I was stuck this way until then. All I could do was try and avoid thinking about it.

"Welcome back, Alexis," Philbert said in greeting as I sat down across from him. "I hope your latest transformation has saddled you with new burdens."

"I'm feeling great," I answered. "I never imagined I could have a waist this tiny before."

"I bet," Philbert agreed. "Few women get this opportunity. And there is still a chance for more. So now I must ask you the all-important question. Are you ready to continue playing Truth or Bimbo College Edition?"

I needed no time to think. I already knew my answer. "Darn right," I said. "Let's play."

8

"Alexis is in for another round," Philbert announced. "That's terrific news. Now the question is will she purposefully throw her next question to try and get herself a body that evens itself out, or will she keep using for more money."

"I need to keep pushing forward on the money," I said. "I have a goal and I need to keep working toward that. And to be honest, it wouldn't be any fun to watch if I was out here purposefully giving incorrect answers. The audience might enjoy seeing a new me, but there wouldn't be any drama in it."

"True," Philbert agreed. "Very true. But now that you are sitting here and comfortable, it is time for your next question. Who was murdered alongside OJ Simpson's estranged wife, Nicole? Was it Johnnie Cochran , Al Cowlings, Ronald Goldman, or Lance Ito?"

I let out an unhappy sigh. This was not the kind of question I wanted to see.

"Hmm," I said, trying to hide my unhappiness and pass it off as being thoughtful. "Unfortunately, the whole OJ murder situation happened before I was born. And I was too busy to watch the documentary about it, so I honestly have no idea."

"Do any of those names sound familiar?" Philbert prompted.

"Johnnie Cochran does," I answered, "but I think that's because he was a lawyer involved in the case. But I'm not even sure of that. I just remember seeing him in a headline in the past couple years, making me think he's not dead."

"Fair enough," Philbert said. "Do you think there are any other names there that you recognize, either for good or for bad?"

"Not a one," I admitted. "Looks like I'm going to be making another guess."

"Guesses aren't always bad," Philbert said. I could tell he was trying to comfort me.

At least I knew I probably wasn't going to end up with a weirdly shaped body for the rest of my life. The odds were against me on this one, just as before.

"I don't know what it is, but I've got a hunch that the answer is Al Cowlings," I finally said. I couldn't explain it, but that name resonated with me for some reason.

"Are you sure that's the answer you want to go with?" Philbert asked.

"Might as well," I said, shrugging my shoulders. "Let's just get it over with. Me debating these things isn't going to get me any closer."

"Very well," Philbert said. "Alexis chooses Al Cowlings."

The music played, the lights flashed and my heart pounded in my chests, wondering if my hunch was correct or if I would be making another trip backstage to visit Dr. Diamond.

"Alexis' choice of Al Cowlings is..." Philbert said, once again pausing for effect. "Incorrect. I'm sorry Alexis, but it looks like you will be moving up another rung on the Bimbo

Board. The correct answer was Ronald Goldman. Cowlings was the owner of the white Bronco that Simpson was chased in."

I wanted to curse, I wanted to hit the monitor, I even wanted to hit Philbert. This was not how I imagined my night would go. I had been ahead, but now I was losing ground again. I had evened things out between the Money Board and the Bimbo Board. Worse, I was only tied because of the deal I had taken with my benefactor to take on all of the facial changes. I was in real trouble now.

"The next Bimbo category is Lower Body," Philbert continued. "This is important for two reasons. One, it will give the benefactor a chance to possibly even out the physical transformations to our dear Alexis, but it also means Alexis is one step away from everyone's favorite category, Breasts."

The audience cheered wildly at the mention of breasts. It really was everyone's favorite category. Even I enjoyed watching that one come about. There was something about the breasts that make the bimbo pop.

When it came to the audience, they almost always went big. And that was completely understandable. Only on a few rare occasions did the contestant end up with something small. And when they did, it was usually due to the audience turning on them if they had been insulting prior or if she already had a large chest and it seemed best to bring her down a size or two.

For me, I was not particularly big, but I also wasn't dealing with the mob mentality of the audience. I was dealing with a single man and his singular choices. That was a major difference.

"The options for Lower Body are," Philbert continued, "Weak Ankles; Partial Hour Glass; Power, Power, and More Power; and Wide Load."

Like with the Upper Body category, Partial Hour Glass

continued to be a crowd favorite. However, all the others had been seen before. Weak Ankles matched up with Wafer Thin. I had seen an audience choose those and then give the contestant beachball-sized breasts. It was overly extreme. The other two categories also lined up with categories from the Upper Body, giving the audience the chance to complete the picture. Not that they always did.

One show chose Strong-Armed Lady and Weak Ankles. It made her look like she was one of those bro lifters that didn't know what leg day meant.

"What do you think of those options?" Philbert asked.

I looked up and made the mistake of making eye contact. My eyes became hooded with lust, but I bit my tongue to keep from licking my lips. Not that I was able to hide my come hither look. I had to remember that was the price I had paid to get a leg up on the Money Board.

"I know I can't speak for my benefactor," I said once I had looked away and let my face return to its now normal confused expression, "but I would personally continue on the path I had started. Each of those options connects to one of the options in the Upper Body category. I would think consistency is a goal here."

"Fair assumption," Philbert said. "However, we won't know what the man has to say until he calls."

As if on cue, the phone in Philbert's pocket rang.

"I love it when the timing works out," Philbert commented as he pulled the phone from his pocket and placed it next to his ear.

I would find out the next part of my fate very soon.

9

"Terrific news," Philbert said as he replaced the phone in his jacket pocket. "Your benefactor agrees with you and wants to continue what he started. He chooses Partial Hour Glass."

I let out a sigh of relief. I hadn't realized I had been holding my breath throughout Philbert's phone call. I was very much glad to hear that my benefactor wanted to keep the hour glass theme with my upper and lower halves. It was hard enough walking around with my old legs and butt when I had a wonderfully toned torso with a waist that made it seem like I was wearing a corset underneath my skin. That was the only explanation.

"It looked like you're happy with your benefactor's choice," Philbert commented.

"I am. I guess I prefer completing the whole picture and now that's exactly what's going to happen."

"Indeed it is," Philbert said. "So it is time to send you backstage again and when we see you again, you'll have a lower body to match your upper body."

The music played me off the stage. I was almost smiling.

As much as it sucked to miss another question, at least I was going to end up looking somewhat normal. Obviously my new waist size was a little extreme, but I wasn't unheard of. The important part was I was going to end up matching.

"There's my favorite show contestant," Dr. Diamond said in greeting. "And you're back so soon. You aren't throwing the game are you? Do you want to become a bimbo that badly?"

"Shut up," I snapped. "I'm not throwing anything."

"Just a hissy fit, I see," Dr. Diamond countered. "Well, never mind about all that. We have some work to do on you. Go stand on your spot. And I'm going to need you to take off the pants and the shoes. I need you naked from the waist down."

As much as I wanted to rebel against my tormentor, I knew the power he held over me and I knew there was nothing I would be able to do to stop him in the end. It was probably bad enough that I snapped at him. He had the power to change my body however he saw fit. I could only imagine what little extras he could throw in, especially after I accused him of doing just that the last time I was here.

"I'm sorry for snapping at you," I apologized as I kicked off my shoes. "I'm just mad at myself for missing another question."

"You're under a lot of stress, I know," Dr. Diamond said. "I don't blame you, although I know of an easy solution to it all."

"What's that?" I asked. I honestly wanted to know how I could improve my situation. I needed to get back to answering questions correctly.

"Just give up and be a bimbo," Dr. Diamond answered. "I have never known a bimbo to feel stress. It's the perfect solution."

"But I don't want to be a bimbo," I countered as I slipped

my show issued pants down my legs, revealing my pussy to this man I despised.

"We'll see how you feel about that later, I'm sure," Dr. Diamond said before changing the subject. "Now, like before, I want you to just relax. Close your eyes if you want. This will only last a few minutes."

I closed my eyes as Dr. Diamond turned on one of his machines. I could feel the warmth of the light from the machine, especially on my legs and around my hips. There was a part of me that wanted to watch. It was the part of me that wished I could have seen this process on the previous shows. Then again, had I seen how all this worked, I might not have been so eager to answer the call for college students to take part. If I hadn't done that, I would have been completely dependent on venture capital to fund my company and I didn't like that idea at all.

"And we're done," Dr. Diamond suddenly announced as the warming light disappeared.

I opened my eyes to see him walking toward the intercom again.

"Alexis is ready for her new shorts and shoes," Dr. Diamond announced.

Meanwhile I stood there looking down at my legs and hips. My legs were nicely toned. It looked like I worked out, even if I actually hadn't. I also found it strange how I didn't feel completely natural standing flat footed. I kept wanting to roll forward onto the balls of my feet and let my heels rise off the ground.

"Ah, you're noticing a little addition I made," Dr. Diamond commented as he approached. "It's one of two additions I've made since you threw a hissy fit earlier. You'll get used to it eventually, but it may take a few hours."

"Hours?" I asked, suddenly fearful that I had been set up.

"Don't worry," Dr. Diamond said. "It's nothing bad. You'll

just find that you prefer wearing high heels from here on out. Your body will adapt quickly enough. But I'm afraid it will be permanent. No amount of physical therapy on your tendons will make it possible to be happy standing flat footed."

"What about the other addition?" I asked.

"That is a favorite of mine, but I'll let you figure that one out on your own," Dr. Diamond answered. "I think you'll see soon enough. I am proud of that ass though. It might be one of my best."

I turned and looked behind me to see my butt sticking out from my backside farther than it ever had before. It either looked like I spent most of my time at the gym doing squats or that I had surgical help.

Reaching behind me, I took a tentative feel of my new butt. It was big and round, but it seemed to be natural. That was the good news. I didn't particularly like the idea of implants. I knew they were likely in my future, given my recent success in the trivia department, but I could hope my benefactor chose a more natural set of breasts for me.

It seemed to take the wardrobe person a minute to arrive. When he did, he came in with a small pair of shorts and a pair of strappy sandals. The shorts were pink to match my top. They also had Thatcher College printed across the back, further enhancing the college aspect of this show.

As for the shoes, they were wedge heels. I supposed that would make them easier to walk in. The cork sole would certainly be more comfortable than a pair of stilettos. I had never been one to wear high heels. I avoided them like the plague, preferring flats or even better yet, skating shoes. There had always been something about skate shoes that I found comfortable, even though I had never used a skateboard in my life.

It didn't take me long to get dressed. The shorts were tight, stretching across my butt. They stretched so much that

I couldn't avoid them pulling a little in the front, especially between my legs. My pussy was on display through the tight material with a prominent camel toe.

"Is there another pair of shorts I can wear?" I asked the guy from wardrobe. "These are a bit tight."

"You'll wear what we give you," the man said before he turned and left in a huff.

"Don't worry about it," Dr. Diamond said. "You look good in those shorts. And guys like to see a camel toe like that. It reminds them that you really are a woman."

I wasn't so sure about that, but I didn't feel like arguing. I had yet to figure out what the other addition was and I feared that more than the camel toe. I would be sitting for most of the show, so it wouldn't really matter anyway.

"It's time to go back out," chem the voice of the burly stagehand.

"Just a moment," I called back. "I need to put on my shoes."

These weren't the kind of shoes I could just slide my feet into and be done. I needed to make sure all the straps were straight before I could go anywhere. I didn't want to fall as soon as I stepped out on the stage.

I had to sit down on the ground to get my shoes on. I would have considered the scrappy wedge sandals cute if I didn't have to wear them on television. If someone else wore them, it would have been a different story.

As soon as they were on the straps had been buckled, I tried to push myself to my feet.

"Whoa," I cried out as I started to fall over.

I hadn't even gotten to my feet and I was already having balance problems. Luckily, the stagehand helped lift me to my feet. He was incredibly strong. I got the sense he barely had to apply any force to lift me to my feet.

"You ready now?" the stagehand asked.

"I think so," I answered.

The man took my by the arm and led me to the door leading out onto the stage. A moment later he shoved me through, leaving me to nearly trip over myself as I found myself back out on the stage and with the crowd cheering for me.

Once I caught my balance, I smiled and waved to the faceless crowd. I was glad I couldn't see them, because I was sure I would be licking my lips and giving them all my best sultry and lustful expression.

However, as I started walking toward my seat across from Philbert, I discovered part of the other addition Dr. Diamond had given me. Each step I took teased my pussy, sending shockwaves up my spine into my brain. If my hair and lips provided small jolts of pleasure, this was significantly more.

For the first time all night, I could honestly say I was horny. This was a level where I would have felt the need to masturbate, assuming I had the privacy to do so. However, on stage with a few hundred people watching me and with cameras filming me, there was no way I could even attempt to satisfy my urges. I could only hope my arousal would dissipate once I was sitting down.

"Look at you," Philbert said, smiling. "That's quite a change. Would you mind giving us a spin? I'm sure our audience members would love to see the new you."

I was still unsteady in my heels, but I couldn't deny Philbert and the rest of the audience a look. This was part of the game, after all. However, as I twirled around, I made sure to keep a hand on the back of my chair the whole time. I didn't want to make a fool of myself by toppling over.

"So what do you think?" Philbert asked as I sat down. "Do you like the changes so far?"

I took a deep breath before I answered, trying to focus my mind away from the heat building between my legs. "Mostly,"

I said. "There have been a few surprises. I guess I have to wear heels now."

I raised one foot to show my wedge heels off to the audience and the cameras.

"They look great on you," Philbert said.

"Thanks. I appreciate that."

"It's been a back and forth game all night," Philbert said. "You are currently tied with four steps on both the Money Board and the Bimbo Board. Are you wanting to call it quits or are you still wanting to play Truth or Bimbo College Edition?"

There was a part of me that wanted to quit. I could be done with all of this. I would lose the money, but I'd still be stuck like this. As much as I generally liked what I saw in the mirror now, I still needed the money for my business. I needed to keep playing so I could reach the top.

"I'm ready to play," I said, making my intentions clear.

10

Philbert smiled as he looked at me. He knew I was going to continue, but I was sure he was instructed to ask every time I returned from the clutches of Dr. Diamond.

There had been a few contestants who quit the show early. To fill the time, the show would film a follow-up and while a few of the women were happy with their decisions, most later regretted not continuing with the game. At least that was what they said in front of the cameras. Who but them knew what they really thought.

However, for myself, I was determined to continue. I wanted the money. I needed the money. And there was nothing that was going to stop me from winning. I would figure out a way, somehow.

"Alexis, you are going for $10,000 on the Money Board," Philbert said. "If you miss this next question, you will reach the Breasts category on the Bimbo Board. How confident do you feel about your chances?"

"I know I can win this," I answered, trying to bolster my confidence. "I have no doubts."

"Very well," Philbert said. "Here's your next question.

Which was the only painting sold by Vincent Van Gogh during his lifetime? Was it The Red Vineyards near Arles, The Starry Night, Van Gogh Self Portrait (1889), or Wheat Field with Crows?"

I wanted to curse. I wanted to hit my monitor. I wanted to storm off the stage, stomping loudly. What the hell kind of question was this? Why did they keep giving me these ridiculously hard questions? I know they gave me some softball computer questions earlier, but this was ridiculous. Was this because I was in college? Did they think I was some genius when it came to trivia?

"I don't even know," I said, throwing up my hands. "I have no guesses. I didn't even know he sold a painting during his lifetime. I know he wasn't popular when he was alive."

"That is true," Philbert said. "His works only became popular and respected after his death. Unfortunately, that doesn't help you answer the question."

"No, it doesn't," I admitted. "Let's see what I can figure. I doubt someone bought his self portrait. That seems dumb to buy from someone who isn't famous. I get the reasons behind painting it, but that's not the sort of thing someone buys to hang on their wall. So that's out."

"Fair enough," Philbert said. "That seems like logical reasoning."

"And the Starry Night should be cut from the list too," I continued. "That's his most famous work. I doubt someone bought that while he was still alive. That means it needs to be the Vineyard painting or the Wheat Field painting."

"Those are the two remaining choices," Philbert said. "If you're right thus far, you've narrowed your choices down to a 50-50 split. Good work."

"Thanks," I said, feeling more confident now. Philbert certainly knew how to build up confidence in the contestants. Then again, he had been hosting various shows for about 40 years now. That alone was impressive. But he had clearly learned a few things over the years.

"I'll be honest," I said. "I don't know much about art. I obviously know about Starry Night, but that's about it. I did see the Doctor Who episode that visited him, but I just remember a painting with some yellow flowers in that one."

"I can't help you there," Philbert said. "I admit, there are some gaps in my television and movie knowledge. I'm only vaguely aware of the Doctor Who franchise."

"I'm not a consistent fan myself," I said. "I just went through a short phase where I watched a bunch of episodes in high school. And again, that doesn't help me here."

I wished I knew more about Van Gogh. I also wished I had access to the internet. I didn't need to look up the answer, but it would have been nice to at least look at the paintings before deciding. If I saw them, I might be able to decide which one I would have bought. That could have provided me with a solution.

"Any more thoughts?" Philbert asked, prompting me to say more.

"I don't know," I said. "I think it comes down to a guess again. I'm trying to think of what I would prefer. Would I prefer looking at a vineyard or at a wheat field? Personally, I think I prefer the latter. There are a bunch of wheat fields near Thatcher College. I've always appreciated their calming beauty when I drive outside of town."

"That must be nice," Philbert said. "It's good to be able to enjoy beautiful things."

"Okay, I think I've decided," I suddenly said. "I'm going to go with the Wheat Fields with Crows as my answer."

"You are certain you want that to be your answer?" Philbert asked. He was giving me one last chance to switch my answer.

"No, but I don't resonate with the other one ass much, so I'm choosing the Wheat Field."

"Very well," Philbert said. "Alexis chooses the Wheat Field with Crows."

The music played, the lights flashed.

"I'm sorry, Alexis," Philbert said, not even bothering to hold for suspense. "The correct answer was the Red Vineyards near Arles."

My head hung low in defeat. That was the closest I had gotten to answering a non-computer question correctly. Was I really so one-dimensional? I thought I knew more than this. I had studied past shows to prepare. I had felt much more capable with the previous questions asked. I had to assume they had made the questions harder for me or something.

"Tough luck on that one," Philbert continued. "You almost had it. But don't fret. You will have more chances to move up the Money Board. In the meantime, however, you have moved up to Breasts on the Bimbo Board."

The crowd cheered loudly at that announcement. It seemed likely many of the audience had been waiting for exactly this moment. Luckily, they couldn't vote this time. I had negotiated that option away from them.

Unfortunately, my fate would lay in the hands of a man I had never met before. He had normal enough tastes thus far, but he could throw me a curveball at any time.

"And the Breasts category is a little different from some of the others," Philbert said. "Rather than four options, there are six. It certainly makes for some interesting results. And those options are Barely There, Just a Handful, Like a Grapefruit, Heavy Hangers, Large and In Charge, and Beachballs."

I could guess the first three options would not appeal to my benefactor. To be financially involved in a show like Truth or Bimbo, he needed to have a love for bimbos and that usually meant being a fan of large breasts. The only question that remained was what best described his preferred shape. There was some size difference between the final three options, but shape was much more obvious in them.

"What do you think of your options?" Philbert asked.

I sighed before answering. "I think I'm going to end up with some large breasts. The only question will be exactly how big and what shape they will take."

"That has certainly been a common theme with our audiences over the past year," Philbert said. "But you never know. Your benefactor may have different ideas."

Philbert's phone rang right on cue again. He fished it out of his pocket and put the phone to his ear.

I had no idea what my benefactor would choose, but I was certain my new breasts would be attention grabbing in some form.

11

"And we have a decision," Philbert announced as he returned his phone to his pocket. "The benefactor has chosen which option he wants to describe Alexis' new breasts."

The crowd cheered. Even though they didn't get a say in this episode, they still loved their breasts. I had a feeling many in the audience were boob men. There didn't seem to be much of a reason to get show tickets otherwise.

"Alexis," Philbert said, addressing me, "your benefactor has chosen your new breasts to be Large and In Charge."

I was actually relieved to hear that. I had already come to terms that my new breasts were going to be large. But I preferred the Large and In Charge look to Heavy Hangers and Beachballs. The former sagged really low on women's chests. That was part of the idea after all. However, it just wasn't for me. I liked the fake look a little bit more.

But Beachball took things too far in the fake direction. They were big and basically spherical. In many cases it literally looked like two beachballs had been attached to a woman's chest underneath the skin. I understood that some people liked that look, but it wasn't for me.

"You seem happy with your benefactor's choice," Philbert said.

"Yeah," I said, taking Philbert's prompt to speak. "I guess if I have to have big boobs, it might as well be those. They'll be fake, but they won't look too fake. And they won't sag down to my belly button when I turn 40 either."

"Those are solid reasons," Philbert said. "I am glad to hear you and your benefactor are basically on the same page."

"I hadn't thought of it that way before," I said. "His last few choices have been solid, I suppose."

"And now it is time to send you backstage to get the new breasts your benefactor has chosen for you," Philbert said. "While Alexis does that, we will take a break. When we return, we will all get to enjoy Alexis' new look. But remember, we can only look. There is no touching, just like at a strip club."

The music played me off the stage as I thought about what Philbert had just said. There had been a few instances where after the breast category was complete, a few members from the audience came out onto the stage from their seats and tried to get handsy with the contestant. The men had all been arrested and charged to the fullest of the law. The studio had pushed for the charges, as by the time the show was over, the contestants usually would have welcomed such an interaction.

"You want me standing again, right?" I asked Dr. Diamond as soon as I arrived in his workshop. It seemed easiest to make me stand. Sitting could lead to strange results. I was certain I was going to be getting some nice big implants without the need for surgery. It had been impressive how none of the changes had required cutting me open. That would have been the norm everywhere else.

"Good guess," Dr. Diamond said. "Usually I like a woman on her knee, but in this case, standing is best."

I avoided showing my annoyance at Dr. Diamond over his crude joke. However, his comment confirmed that he was exactly as big of a creep as I had figured he was. My intuition when it came to trivia answers might not be very good, but my intuition when it came to creeps like Dr. Diamond was perfect.

I took my spot on the X and then pulled off my tank top. I didn't know if the top would fit after I had been given my new breasts. I figured it was best not to find out.

"Thank you for taking your top off," Dr. Diamond said. "You might as well get used to doing that. You'll have lots of practice in the future, I'm sure."

I wanted to chew him out, but I had learned my lesson for that already. Just walking off the stage had left me nearly weak in the knees. How was I supposed to live with this constant arousal? It seemed no matter what I did, it would be there. I could only imagine being in the middle of a meeting as CEO and suddenly telling everyone that I needed to take a break. After learning of my participation on Truth or Bimbo, they would all know why I needed the break and what I would be doing. I would need to soundproof my office too. My employees didn't need to hear me get myself off every few hours.

"I have to say," Dr. Diamond continued once he saw I was not going to snap at him, "I think your benefactor has great taste. This is my favorite category and he chose my favorite option. Your new sweater puppies are going to precede you wherever you go and they will dominate every interaction you have with people. They're going to be like magnets, drawing everyone's gaze down into a deep valley of cleavage."

"I can choose to cover them up," I countered, finally succumbing to his bait.

Dr. Diamond only laughed.

I had seen some contestants tugging at their tops after getting their new breasts. I began to wonder if that was Dr. Diamond's doing. Maybe he somehow made it necessary for the women to show off their new breasts. I didn't know and I didn't want to know. Unfortunately, I was afraid I would be finding out soon enough.

"Here we go," Dr. Diamond said as he positioned the machine in front of me. A moment later I was bathed in the familiar warm light, this time specifically focusing on my chest.

I closed my eyes after that, not wanting to watch. However, I could feel a weight growing on my chest. Two weights to be precise. I could feel my breasts ballooning out, growing larger and larger, the skin getting tighter and tighter, until I was certain they would pop.

And then just like that, the warm light shut off. I opened my eyes and looked down. I couldn't see my feet as I stood there. All I could see were a pair of large breasts. They were too big and too high on my chest to be real.

I tentatively reached up with my hands and felt the taut flesh. They were softer than I had imagined, but I could feel the foreign material under the skin. I definitely had implants now.

My next thought was whether there might be some way to hide my new breasts. I figured I could have them taken out if I wanted after the show. I would have the money and it would probably cost less than $10,000. That was tiny compared to the full $100 million prize.

"You can put your top back on," Dr. Diamond said. "That one should be stretchy enough to handle your new girls.

Unless you want to keep it off and give them some more air to breathe?"

I didn't like Dr. Diamond's suggestion, so I started to pull my top back on, covering up my now large boobs. Really, at this size, they were tits. I let the word roll around in my head. It certainly was easy to roll off the tongue, but it also felt a bit degrading. Could I really call them tits? It made me feel a little dirty, even if the word did properly describe my new boobs.

Pulling the tank top down over my tits took a bit more work than I had figured it would. One, I had tits the size of some melons I could buy at the grocery store. They were almost as big as my head. It took a lot of effort to squeeze them into my tank top, but I finally managed.

However, pulling the rough fabric across my nipples sent happy waves of pleasure up into my brain and down into my pussy. I could feel my juices building up inside of me at the sensation. Worse, once my tank top was in place, my hard nipples poked through. The top was not stretched so thin where you could see the purple of my areolas and nipples, but you could certainly see my nipples tenting the fabric.

I walked over to the mirror to get a better look at myself. My jaw nearly hit the floor as I saw the complete package that was me. I looked like a total bimbo. Big lips, big tits and big ass; I matched all around. What was more, to account for the extra volume of my tits, the tank top bunched up around my midriff and fully exposed my belly button. I was going to have to buy a whole new wardrobe to account for the change in my body.

And, like I had seen before, I found myself tugging on my neckline, trying to pull it lower and expose more of my cleavage. Dr. Diamond had done it again.

"What do you think, my dear?" Dr. Diamond asked as he

stood off to the side to enjoy the view. "I think you are perfectly balanced. I'm sure your benefactor will love that."

Up until this point, I had assumed I would win the game and take home the big prize. However, looking at my reflection, going over everything that had changed with my body, I had a sudden sense of dread. It seemed hopeless now. I was going to lose.

And worse, after the Breasts category came mental transformations. Those would mess with my head and there would be nothing I could do once my sense of self had been altered. I would be forever changed.

"They're big," I finally said. That was definitely true. They were big. I had big tits now. And they were bigger than I could have ever imagined. Seeing them, I had a hard time believing they were a part of me. However, just touching them was enough to remind me that yes, this was who I was now. I would just have to learn to deal with it.

That was all I said to Dr. Diamond. I didn't want to give him the satisfaction of knowing how far he had pushed me. I turned away from the mirror and walked toward the door, letting my hips sway as I stopped fighting my shoes, knowing that each step I took would leave me more and more aroused.

"You ready?" asked the burly stagehand.

"I think so," I answered.

"Then get out there."

I walked out onto the stage to big cheers from the crowd. They whooped and hollered as I made my way to my seat. I knew they liked what they saw. And oddly, there was a part of me that liked that fact. I had never been particularly popular with men. Then again I was too focused on my studies and work to let myself get distracted by romance and sex.

"You are looking great," Philbert said as I sat down. "The

crowd certainly loves you. What do you think of your new breasts?"

"They're big," I said, not knowing what else to say.

"That they are," Philbert agreed. "But now it's time to turn our attention back to the game. Are you ready to continue playing Truth or Bimbo College Edition?"

I needed a moment to consider. A part of me had been confident I wouldn't get this far. But now that I was here, I was beginning to really doubt myself. However, leaving would mean I would leave with no money. At the very least, I needed something to pay for some new clothes. Nothing I had at home in my closet would fit the new me. That alone decided my fate.

"Philbert," I finally said. "I'm ready to play."

As I sat there across from Philbert, I could not help but think about how much my life had changed in such a short amount of time. I doubted my own parents would recognize me now. The long blonde hair, the button nose, the plump lips, the big ass, the tiny waist and the giant tits made me look like an entirely different person.

But I didn't just look different. I felt different too. I felt as if my entire body had been primed for sex. Licking my lips, brushing my hair, even going for a walk turned me on. I had enough self control to keep myself from doing something embarrassing, but how long would that last? From here on out, the changes would primarily be psychological. I had little doubt Dr. Diamond and his machines would begin to little down my self control until I simply couldn't stop myself from doing something I might come to regret.

However, all of this made me more determined to win the game. I was not going to let myself be turned into a bimbo. I might have looked the part, but I refused to let myself act the part too. Somehow I would win this thing.

"Are you ready for your next question?" Philbert asked

me. "Remember you are still chasing after the $10,000 level on the Money Board, but you risk moving up to Speech on the Bimbo Board."

"I'm ready," I said, trying to relax myself so I could better focus. I knew I would have a chance if I just relaxed and thought through the questions.

"Here we go," Philbert said. "What was the first movie to be rated PG-13? Was it Gremlins, Indiana Jones and the Temple of Doom, Red Dawn, or The Terminator?"

This I should have known. I had seen all of those movies. The only problem was I never paid attention to their ratings. Somehow I figured Indiana Jones had something to do with the PG-13 rating. It was a gut feeling, but my gut hadn't been doing very good at being right lately. All of my gut choices had been wrong and sent me back for another meeting with Dr. Diamond.

"That's a good question," I said as I tried to find a way to tackle the question. "I'm trying to remember what the movies were rated. I've seen all of them."

"They all came out in the mid-eighties, as I recall," Philbert said. "Hopefully the producers won't see that information as being a hint."

"Oh, I know roughly when they came out," I said. "Admittedly, they all came out long before I was born. But I went through a phase where I liked to watch a lot of old movies."

"That's an interesting comment," Philbert said. "I never thought of any of those movies as old. Then again, age is more than a number."

"Sorry," I said, suddenly embarrassed for an entirely different reason. Yes, Philbert was significantly older than me, but I had essentially called him old by proxy. "They're old to me. Old and young are relative concepts, you know."

Philbert smiled. I wasn't looking at his face, but I could

just tell. "Right you are. But please don't let a discussion of age distract you from your deliberations."

"Okay, well," I started to say, trying to find the words I wanted to use as my brain worked overtime to try and find some way of dissecting the questions and its possible answers. "I'm pretty sure The Terminator was rated R. It just seems far too violent to fit as PG-13. So that one's out. And somehow, I'm pretty sure Gremlins was PG, but I'm not sure how I know that. It's a maybe."

I was second guessing myself, which was not a good place to be. However, I needed to move forward. I could come back to Gremlins again later if I needed to.

"But if I leave that aside, I still have Red Dawn and Indiana Jones. I just don't know which one it would be."

"You seem to have it down to two," Philbert said. "That's good."

"Two and a half, really," I countered. "There's something about Gremlins that I'm forgetting. It also doesn't help that Temple of Doom is the Indiana Jones movie I most ignore, after Crystal Skull, of course. They never should have made that movie."

Philbert laughed. I smiled at hearing it. He always had a way of lightening the mood.

"You're not just a computer program and tech entrepreneur, but a film critic too," Philbert joked.

"Something like that," I agreed. "I had a friend that was a big movie buff. He would bring over movies to watch every weekend. I saw a lot of movies that way."

I turned my attention back to the question at hand. I was missing something. I knew that. However, I just couldn't get Indiana Jones out of my head. It didn't help that Harrison Ford looked pretty sexy back then.

"You know what," I said, growing tired of trying to decide between Indiana Jones and Red Dawn. "I'm going to go with

Indiana Jones and the Temple of Doom. I have a gut feeling about that. I'm not sure what my gut is trying to tell me, but there it is."

"You're sure you want to select Indiana Jones and the Temple of Doom as your answer," Philbert asked.

"As sure as I'll ever be without knowing the answer."

"Alexis chooses Indiana Jones and the Temple of Doom."

The music began to play and the lights flashed. At this point, it no longer held the same sway over me as before. I had become used to it. Or maybe I was just out of adrenaline, my body unable to feel the suspense.

"The first PG-13 movie was…" Philbert said with a long pause, "not Indiana Jones and the Temple of Doom."

For a moment I was excited, thinking that I had guessed correctly. But then I realized he had used the word not. I had been wrong again.

I threw my head back and looked up toward the ceiling where the lights hung. I closed my eyes and cursed my luck. This was not going my way. I had moved into the psychological categories of the Bimbo Board.

"For everyone who is curious," Philbert continued, "the first PG-13 movie was Red Dawn. Alexis, you were correct that The Terminator was rated R. However, both Gremlins and Indiana Jones and the Temple of Doom were rated PG. Both movies are considered catalysts to introducing the PG-13 rating, with the Indiana Jones film receiving most of the credit."

That must have been what my gut was trying to tell me. Apparently I didn't know how to listen to my own hunches.

"Not the round you wanted to have, was it?" Philbert asked.

"No, it wasn't. I thought I was on the right track. Maybe I'm just too impulsive."

"Being impulsive is not always a bad thing," Philbert said.

"And you were close on this. You again narrowed the list down to two, but that still left you with a 50-50 chance and those can always go either way."

"I guess you're right," I said, trying to see the bright side of the situation.

"Unfortunately, it is now time to announce your next step up on the Bimbo Board," Philbert said. "The next rung on the Bimbo Board is Speech. This will change the words you use, without you being able to control it, almost like a filter and translation program that sits between your brain and your mouth. However, our producers believe that over time, your brain will adapt and you'll begin to think using the same speech pattern that you hear yourself using."

I took a deep breath to try and calm myself. This was not my night. I could see that now. But I was also far enough into the game that I wanted to see it through. I would keep playing until the end, hoping I could take home the grand prize.

"That's a scary thought," I said. "I can't imagine how my thinking would change just from hearing myself speak."

"I'm no expert myself," Philbert said. "I am simply parroting some of the information I have been told. I'm sure there is a psychological experiment to address this issue, but it is beyond my scope."

I couldn't remember what speech options Jordan had been given in the first episode. I vaguely recalled her frequently talking about sex afterward though. I would find out what would happen soon enough, once Philbert finished introducing the category.

"But back to your new speaking style," Philbert said. "The options are Only When Spoken To, Like Totally a Valley Girl, A Foul Mouth, and Sex on the Brain. What do you think of your options, Alexis?"

Hearing Sex on the Brain, I knew that had been Jordan's

result. She kept slipping sexual innuendos into her sentences and finding other ways to reference sex and sexual acts. It was amazing they even let that kind of thing on television.

As for the other categories, I had seen them all at some point and they all seemed pretty self-explanatory. My only real concern was A Foul Mouth. Whenever that was picked, the producers were forced to bleep a great deal of the contestant's language from that point onward.

But as for me, I didn't want to always be the person using bad language or turning everything I said into a sexual reference. I couldn't be an effective company leader if that were the case. Even I would want to fire myself.

"I guess one of the first two," I said. "I've never been big on cursing, so I would prefer not to suddenly start now and I don't think I could be a good tech company founder with every sentence I uttered was laced with sexual innuendos."

"Those are good points," Philbert said. "How would you feel if you could only speak once someone had spoken to you?"

"I wouldn't like it," I admitted. "But I could live with it."

"Well, it's that time of the show where we wait for a call from Alexis' benefactor," Philbert said as his phone began to ring.

He pulled the phone from his pocket and placed it to his ear. Now I just had to wait to see my future fate.

Philbert hung up the phone and returned it to his pocket. He then looked at me for a moment before he began to speak.

"Your benefactor says he had a hard time deciding which option to choose. However, he took your suggestions into account and has selected Like Totally a Valley Girl."

Overall, that had been a popular option, however, I noticed it more often earned second place in the voting than winning outright. And I could understand that. Throwing in likes and totallys and other Valley Girl speaking patterns was classic Southern California bimbo, but it could also get annoying.

"What do you think of that choice?" Philbert asked.

"It is what it is," I said. "At least I already planned to start my tech company in California where such speaking styles are a little more mainstream."

"That's a nice way to think about it," Philbert said. "But now it's time to send you backstage. And I'm sure your bene-factor, our studio audience, and all our viewers at home will be excited to hear you speak when you return. I know I will be."

"Thanks," I said, but the bumper music had already begun to play. I took that as my cue to stand up, step off the dais, and walk off the stage.

Dr. Diamond greeted me at the door to his workshop, rubbing his hands and looking at me with eagerness.

"Now the real fun begins," Dr. Diamond said. "As much fun as the physical transformation process is, I think I like the psychological transformations even more. There's nothing quite like mucking about in a woman's brain, changing the way she thinks. There are so many possibilities. I could switch one fact in your brain, let's say turning the taste of chocolate from something you like and enjoy to something you dislike and hate. Just think about how that one difference could change your whole life."

"No more mochas at lunch, I suppose," I said.

"Exactly," Dr. Diamond said. "And that's not even the half of it. I could make your brain crave the taste of cum. Within a couple weeks you would be sucking down so many loads of cum everyday, you might be able to skip meals."

I shuddered at the thought of becoming a cum slut like that, of giving myself over to a craving, and addition, that would see me as a sexual plaything for the rest of my life.

"Could you just get on with this?" I asked moodily. I was getting tired of making frequent trips to visit Dr. Diamond in what amounted to a bimbo factory. I just wanted to get this latest transformation over with so I could go back out and try to win the game. And maybe after a few years of deep practice and could train myself to talk like a normal human being again.

"Take it easy," Dr. Diamond said. "Take it easy. I'm just about ready for you. Let's have you sit down in the chair for this. No need to make you stand while I'm making changes in your brain."

I followed Dr. Diamond toward the chair where I had begun the process to become the woman I now appeared to be. I sat down and waited as he fiddled around with equipment behind me. I didn't bother to try and look. To be honest, at this point, I didn't want to know how all this worked. I just wanted this whole ordeal to be over as soon as possible.

"If you'll lean your head forward for a moment," Dr. Diamond said as he approached me. "I just need to fit this helmet over your head."

I did as I was asked, leaning forward. A moment later, everything went dark as a full-sized helmet was brought down over my head. There was even an attachment that went around my neck, I guess to hold it on my head. Not that I planned to take it off unless Dr. Diamond directed me to.

I had come to terms with my situation. I wasn't going to fight Dr. Diamond or anyone else. I would keep going and keep my head held high. Whatever happened tonight, I would learn to live with it.

"And now it's time to switch everything on," Dr. Diamond announced.

The helmet began to hum and vibrate ever so slightly. More importantly, lights flashed before my eyes. Even after I closed them, I could still see the lights. Then there was the heat around my neck. I had no idea what was happening.

Nor did I have any idea of how long I sat there. Time lost its meaning as Dr. Diamond's helmet performed its work on me. I didn't feel any different, but I was sure whatever he tried to do would be successful. I was no guinea pig. This show had been running for a year now and they had worked out the kinks. There was no way any of this equipment was dangerous unless it was used improperly. I was certain of that. Liability is a funny thing that way.

Eventually the lights stopped, the hum ended and the hot sensation around my neck dissipated. A moment later, I found myself blinking rapidly as my eyes adjusted to the bright lights in Dr. Diamond's backstage workshop.

"How do you feel?" Dr. Diamond asked.

"Um," I started to say. "I'm, like, totally good."

I clapped my hands over my mouth after the words came pouring out. Not only were my words not what I intended to say, but my voice sounded different. It was higher pitched and softer. I had a feeling my presence in the boardroom would take a hit. So too would my presence in a press conference.

What I had meant to say was simply, "I'm good." That was it. Instead, there was an um, a like and a totally, mixed in. None of those additions were intended. The speech filter worked. No matter what I wanted to say, from here on out, something else would come spilling out of my mouth instead.

"That's good," Dr. Diamond said. "I wouldn't want to think I had caused you undue distress."

I wanted to tell Dr. Diamond off. He had done more than changed how I speak, which was bad enough. He had changed my voice too. Now I didn't even sound like I used to. There was no way people would recognize me anymore. I would even sound different on the phone now.

I nearly snapped back at his last comment. I certainly wanted to, however, I was afraid of what I would say. The Valley Girl style of speech was so varied, that I didn't know what exactly would come pouring out of my mouth if I tried to say anything. I was sure Dr. Diamond would just end up laughing at me. And worse, he might choose to take it out on me the next time I saw him. I could only imagine how he could screw with me as he gave me new hobbies, which was the next Bimbo Board level.

"I'm gonna, like, go back on stage now," I finally said, looking for an excuse to get away from my tormentor.

"Have fun," was all Dr. Diamond said in response, his smile wide, like he knew something I didn't. All I could hope was I would never find out.

"You ready?" the burly stagehand asked me as I approached him.

"Like, totally," I said, followed by a giggle.

Again, I clamped my hand over my mouth. This time I was not surprised by what I said or how I said it, but in the giggle that escaped my lips after I said it.

"Like, hold on a sec, k?" I said as I backed away from the stagehand so I could have a moment to compose myself.

"Shit, shit, shit, shit," I said as I paced back and forth, just out of sight of the stagehand. Thankfully I could still curse. That was good to know. But giggling? That seemed to be a step too far in my opinion. Now I not only looked like a bimbo, but I sounded like one too. It had become even more important that I win this, because if I didn't, there was no way I would be taken seriously by a venture capitalist. It was hard enough to begin with, which led me to sign up for Truth or Bimbo in the first place. But now, if I failed, it would be even worse.

I stopped for a moment, realizing that I was walking much more easily as I paced back and forth. I kicked my foot out a little in front of me, just so I could see over my tits. I was still wearing the high heels the wardrobe department had given me. I should have been struggling to walk, especially after the radical change in my center of gravity with my big tits. Yes, despite all of that, it all felt natural.

Did Dr. Diamond change that about me too? Did he alter how I perceived my balance? In a way, I needed to thank him, because everything felt much more natural now. However, I didn't like the idea that he was mucking around in my head and making additional changes. He wasn't supposed to do that. Then again, if he didn't do that, it just meant that my brain had quickly adapted to the new dimensions of my body. Either Dr. Diamond was an ass, which I already knew he was, or I was more in tune with my body than I ever could have imagined.

"It's time to get out there," the stagehand said as he stepped away from the stage door.

"I'm, like, totally coming," I called back, my voice coming out sweet as honey.

It was weird to hear my voice sound so different. I couldn't have mimicked this way of speaking before, even if I had tried. It was one more thing I would need to get used to. It would either take a few minutes or weeks. I had no idea.

I returned to the stage door and paused for a moment to compose myself. I stood up straight, even pulling my shoulders back. That effectively caused me to thrust my tits out. The stagehand seemed to enjoy that. I could see him staring down into my exposed cleavage out of the corner of my eyes. However, as I stood there, I closed my eyes and tried to center myself. I knew my speaking would be off. I would just have to live with that. But I needed to focus and work to answer these questions correctly. If my gut was going to be wrong all the time, maybe it was time I stop trusting my gut and choose the opposite. That seemed the most logical thing to do.

"I'm, like, ready," I said as I exhaled and opened my eyes. After all that had happened to me, I still was still proud. I had come a long way and I would continue to fight and do everything I could to win this game and launch the biggest tech company in the world.

I stepped out onto the stage and walked with confidence

as I approached the dais. I smiled at the crowd and waved. I let my body do its thing. I didn't fight it. I let my hips sway back and forth as I walked in my high heels. I let my tits bounce and bound inside my tight tank top. My hair, still in a ponytail, swished back and forth as I made my way to my seat.

The audience cheered. They whooped and hollered and clapped for me. I even got a few wolf whistles and I was pretty sure I heard another marriage proposal. That made me smile even more. There were some advantages to looking like a bimbo. Men were so much easier to manipulate. And given how I now talked, they wouldn't even notice how I was playing them.

"Welcome back, Alexis," Philbert said joyfully. "Tell me, what do you think of this latest change?"

I sat down and took a moment to figure out how I wanted to answer Philbert's question.

"It's, like, totally different," I said. "And my voice is, like, super sexy now."

The crowd clapped and cheered, clearly happy with my new voice. I might not dominate in the boardroom, but I was beginning to realize I had other powers at my disposal. Feminine seduction was a powerful tool when wielded correctly.

Philbert chuckled at my answer. "Yes, I must say it is. I don't think there is a better way to put it. Clearly you get some enjoyment out of all of this. You're smiling."

I giggled again. "Smiling is, like, totally nice, don't you think?"

I wasn't a fan of the giggling, but I would just have to live with it. I figured it wouldn't hurt me with this crowd.

"I couldn't have put it better myself," Philbert said."But turning our attention back to the game, I have one question to ask. Are you ready to continue playing Truth or Bimbo College Edition?"

"Like, of course I am," I said, punctuating my statement with another giggle. I couldn't control them, but I had to admit, I had good timing. The crowd cheered at my statement. I was going to continue playing to the end and I was pretty sure everyone in the building understood that fact.

It was weird sitting there across from Philbert and realizing how little progress I had made in the game. It was becoming increasingly clear I was going to lose. And now that I both looked and talked like a bimbo, I didn't see that I had much choice but to continue.

Thinking back, I had no idea what I was thinking, believing I could win this game. No one else had been able to do it in the year the show had been on the air. That is, of course, that they aired all the episodes that had been filmed. I wouldn't put it past the producers to both rig the game and rig what the home viewing audience saw.

All I could think about was how I had just been young and foolish in all of this. There was no way I could win this game. But there was still hope. I knew that for sure. There was hope I could pull this out. And if I didn't, I would try to earn as much money as I could to help give me a better life in the future.

"Alexis," Philbert said. "You're chasing after $10,000. But if you fail, the next Bimbo Board category will be Hobby. You are certain you want to continue playing?"

"Like, totally," I said, punctuating my affirmation with a giggle. "And I'm gonna, like, be super good and totally win everything."

I was babbling. I couldn't help it. All I had wanted to say was, "Yes, I'm certain." Unfortunately, it seemed like I would forevermore use lots of words, most of which were just filler material, to say the most basic of things.

As much as I wanted to fight it, I knew I had no control over it. My words would always be bubbly and make me sound like a complete idiot. My only fear was after hearing myself speak this way for long enough, it might change my thought patterns. Someday I might legitimately speak this way, without having a filter change my words. They would flow freely, because those were the words I intended to use.

"I'm sure everyone here is glad to hear it," Philbert said. "I know I am. It has been a pleasure playing Truth or Bimbo College Edition with you, but there is still so much more of the game to play."

"That's, like, super nice of you to say."

I hadn't even meant to say anything. The words came tumbling out of my mouth before I even thought of a response. It was made worse, because I looked at Philbert as I said it. I batted my eyelashes before letting my eyelids fall to a hooded state. I licked my lips seductively, sending another tingle down my spine.

I looked away as soon as I could manage. My pussy felt like it was buzzing between my legs. How was I supposed to think about stupid trivia questions when my body wanted to betray me? I wanted nothing more than to stick my fingers down my shorts. I needed relief. My arousal continued to grow, leaving me wanting more and more.

It even would have been reasonable to let my hands fall between my legs, giving myself a few tempting strokes through my shorts. But even that would be bad. I could imagine myself sitting there with a room of several hundred people, all of them watching me, as I threw my head back as I pleasured myself.

It was an obscene image, but I could see myself doing it in my mind, making it all the worse. There was a growing part of me that seemed to no longer care about modesty decorum. That part of me only cared about satisfying the growing urges inside of me.

"Focus," I told myself, not letting myself speak, not knowing what would pour out from my lips. But my mind was still mine. That was something I could work with. As long as my mind was my own, I still had a chance.

"Are you ready for your next question?" Philbert asked.

I didn't answer at first. I was lost in my own thoughts, trying to focus, only to realize as Philbert spoke, that I wasn't really listening to him or paying attention to what was happening outside my own mind.

"Oh, like, yeah," I finally said. "I'm totally ready."

Philbert chuckled at my response. "You may be my favorite contestant we've had on this show. But back to the game. You have a question to answer. In Swedish, a skvader is a rabbit with what unusual feature? Is it a forked tongue, gills, a hook or wings?"

If I didn't already look surprised at seeing this next question, I certainly did now. I had never heard of a skvader. I had no reference point. Clearly it was a fictional creature. That much was obvious. I had never heard of a rabbit with any of those features before. But there were so many possibilities.

"Um, like," I started to say, trying to stall for time while I came up with something to say. "I totally haven't heard of a skvader before."

"Not everyone has," Philbert responded. "If you don't know, I guess you'll have to guess."

"Um, so, like, I don't think it's gills," I said thinking out loud, although speaking words different from what I thought. "And a hook sounds super weird. It's gonna be, like, wings or the forked tongue."

"That seems reasonable," Philbert said. "If you're correct, you're down to a 50-50 chance again."

"Ooh, yeah," I said, suddenly giddy. "I, like, totally didn't think of that. You're super smart."

It took me a moment to recover from that sudden outburst. I hadn't meant to say anything, but the words and emotion poured out of me without any sense of control. Oddly, there was a certain amount of pleasure in uttering those words.

It was not specifically a sexual pleasure. This was more deep-seeded, less superficial than pure sexual pleasure, like I felt every time I licked my lips or brushed my hair. It was pleasurable to my soul, reaching the very core of my being. It was exhilarating, yet scary too. I honestly did not know what to make of it.

"Do you have any thoughts about how to answer the question?" Philbert asked. My silence had once again gotten to the point where I needed prompting to continue speaking.

"Well, um, like, I don't know, you know?" I said, turning a useless statement into a question.

As Philbert silently chuckled at me and my new way of speaking, I tried to decide which of my remaining two options seemed most likely. I had narrowed the choices down to a forked tongue and wings. Both seemed possible. Unfortunately I had no experience with Swedish, so I couldn't tackle the problem from an etymology perspective. I couldn't dissect the word.

I tried imagining this creature with either of the two additions. Wings made sense, but I just couldn't imagine a flying rabbit. On the other hand, I could see where a rabbit with a forked tongue might be noteworthy. I could imagine it being seen as some devilish creature.

"I'm gonna, like, choose the forked tongue one," I finally said before I burst out into a burst of giggles. It seemed the only thing I was missing at the moment was a big wad of chewing gum. I hated to imagine how that would feel if I blew a bubble with it. Even if the gum on my lips wasn't an issue, I knew licking up a popped bubble off my kips would drive me crazy with arousal.

"You're sure?" Philbert asked. "It's not too late to change your mind."

"Yeah, I'm, like, super sure," I answered. "That's totally gonna be, like, my answer."

"Very well," Philbert said. "Alexis chooses forked tongue."

The music began to play and the lights strobed. I could feel my heart rate increase slightly. This was my chance to finally get another question right and get back in control of this game. All I needed was one right answer to regain some momentum.

"This time," Philbert said, "Alexis is wrong again. I'm sorry, but the correct answer was wings. The skvader is a rabbit with wings. Once again, you guessed incorrectly."

"That's, like, not fair," I pouted. I couldn't help it. I wanted to be right. I wanted to finally answer a question correctly. This was not how I expected the night to go. Even though I knew I was likely going to end up as a bimbo, I still held out hope that I could turn things around and win outright.

"It is what it is," Philbert said. "And in this case, the correct answer was not the one you selected. Therefore it is time to move up the Bimbo Board. Your next category is Hobby. Anything you want to say before I present you with the options for your benefactor to choose from?"

"Like, no," I said as I folded my arms under my tits and continued to pout. Of course, in doing so, my arms pushed my tits up into an even greater display of cleavage. And to make matters worse, my movement caused the fabric of my top to scrape and rub against my nipples, making them even harder and sending another jolt of pleasure down into my pussy.

I could feel the moisture building up between my legs. It wouldn't be long before I would be sporting a wet spot there. I had seen it happen before. Other women in my position on this show had grown too horny to hide their own arousal.

But I couldn't think about that now. I needed to focus on the game and find out what my new hobby would be.

"All right then," Philbert said. "Here are the categories for your newest hobby. There is Exploring Kink, Fashion Expert, Home Ec Perfection, and Anything Outdoors."

I had forgotten all of what Jordan had faced in that first show. I remembered how the audience selected Fashion Expert. From that point on, she always looked phenomenal and completely on trend. It made me a little jealous, knowing how untrendy I was.

However, there was a chance all that would change. Interestingly, I had never seen Anything Outdoors selected before. I had no idea what it would give me, whether it was a love for spending time outside or if it made me want to have sex outside, I hoped I never found out.

"Any thoughts on what you'd like your benefactor to select for you?" Philbert asked.

"I've always, like, wondered what Fashion Expert would feel like," I said. "It seems super cool."

"Ah, yes," Philbert said. "That has been a popular one. But really it all comes down to your benefactor."

A moment later, Philbert's phone rang. He placed the phone to his ear and listened. I could only hope the news coming from the other end was good.

15

"It seems we have another deal being offered," Philbert said. "Alexis, your benefactor is offering you a step up on the Money Board if you take on all four Hobby options."

I looked up at the two boards. I was falling behind on the Money Board. That was a major problem. I hadn't answered a question correctly in a long time. But, sitting at $1,000 wasn't going to get me very far at the end of the game. That would only afford me a couple outfits to fit my new body. I would need more if I was going to replace my wardrobe. And I'd have to replace my wardrobe if Fashion Expert was chosen for me. My basic sweatshirt and jeans look would not pass muster if I became an expert on fashion.

"I'll, like, totally take the deal," I said, knowing it would help me in the long run. Either I would have more money at the end of the game, or it was one step closer to winning if I got myself on a run.

"Fantastic," Philbert said. "Alexis, we will once again be sending you backstage. When you return, you will have a whole new set of interests. I hope you enjoy them as much as we will."

I didn't say anything before the music started. That was my cue to leave the stage, which I promptly did. My ass swayed from side to side as I walked off the stage. I couldn't help it, given my high heels and new proportions. However, just the short walk off the stage and into Dr. Diamond's workshop left me turned on more than I could ever remember being before.

Sex was not a big part of my life. I had, on occasion, been with a man, but my libido had never been turned up so high. Usually my fingers or my trusty vibrator were enough to get me through a few of those instances when my body begged for attention. But those incidents were rare.

Now, however, I felt like a walking sex bomb. I didn't know how much longer I could go before I was begging Dr. Diamond, the burly stagehand, or Philbert to either fuck me or let me play with myself. It was getting bad and every step I took only made it worse.

"Welcome back," Dr. Diamond said. "How's my favorite games how contestant doing?"

"I super hate you," I said. "You and, like, everyone here are totally awful."

I couldn't tell what was causing it, but I felt moody. One moment I was focused and nice and the next moment I was irritable and unhappy. It didn't help that the more aroused I got, the harder it was to focus and the more I wanted to hit someone. At the moment, that someone was Dr. Diamond as he leered at me with his evil gaze.

"All you girls go through that phase," Dr. Diamond said. "And you all get over it eventually. You need to stop fighting all this and just embrace it. You'll be so much happier if you just give in and become the bimbo you were meant to be."

I didn't say a word to that. I simply walked over to the chair and threw myself down into it.

"Just, like, get it over with," I finally said after Dr.

Diamond stood back and watched me with a smirk on his face. We both knew what was happening to me. Half of my situation could be attributed to him. The way my body kept finding ways to get turned on was his fault. He gave me the sensitive lips and hair, he gave me the rock-hard nipples, and he was behind how each step I took served to turn me on more and more.

"You need to smile more," Dr. Diamond said as he approached with the helmet. "I know women hate it when men tell them that, but I hope you'll eventually find how true it is. All girls like you should smile. You should be happy. I mean, just imagine how much life for you will be improved by embracing your bimbo nature. Every woman should be a bimbo. Every woman wants to be a bimbo. Most of them just don't know it yet."

I bristled at Dr. Diamond's archaic attitude, but I wasn't about to argue with him. I was in his domain and he had the power to punish me in the strangest of ways for talking back to him. I had already learned it was best to just let him work.

"Lean forward, please," Dr. Diamond said.

I leaned my head forward to give him better access to place the helmet on my head. Once it was in place, I relaxed again, sitting back knowing it would all be over soon enough.

"And here we go," Dr. Diamond announced before the lights began to flash before my eyes.

I closed my eyes. It was a natural response to the lights. However, closing them did not block out the light. The lights burned themselves through my eyelids, seeming to find a way directly into my mind.

As I sat there, I could tell that something was changing. I could almost feel my synapses rearranging themselves, creating new pathways that would forever change the way my mind worked, the way I thought.

I lost all track of time as my new hobbies were embedded

in my brain. The only consolation to my predicament was the fact I had moved up to $10,000 on the Money Board. That was real money that could actually buy something.

And then, just like that, the lights turned off. A moment after that, Dr. Diamond lifted the helmet off my head.

"How do you feel?" he asked.

It took me a moment to fully return to my senses. I felt a little dazed. It probably had something to do with how much Dr. Diamond was mucking about inside my head.

"Um, like, fine, I guess," I finally answered.

"It will probably take your mind a few minutes, at least, to adapt to all the changes I had to make," Dr. Diamond explained. "I've never had to add four hobbies at once. But there's at least one thing I'd like you to do before I send you back out there."

"Like, what?" I asked.

"Just stand in front of the mirror for me."

I pushed myself up from the chair, noticing my short fingernails for the first time. That wasn't right. I shouldn't have short nails. I needed long fashionable nails. I almost couldn't believe I had allowed my appearance to drop to such poor standards.

I was able to put my short nails out of my mind long enough to walk over to the mirror to look at my reflection. I felt as if I was seeing myself for the first time. At the very least, I saw myself in a whole new light. My perspective had completely changed. I was attractive, yes, but my standards had changed.

"Fuck, I'm, like, almost perfect," I said, enjoying my reflection for the first time in my life.

I reached up and ran my fingers through my hair. I shuddered at the tingle that ran down my spine into my pussy, but I ignored it. I had more important things to do. Namely, I needed to take my hair out of the ponytail. It was fine to put it up like that when working out, but the rest of the time, I knew I needed to either wear my hair down or completely up. For now, I decided down would be best.

Removing the scrunchie from my hair sent several more tingles down my spine. I managed to once again ignore them.

"Do you, like, have any styling product I can, you know, use?" I asked Dr. Diamond.

Dr. Diamond went to the intercom and called for the wardrobe man to return. He then turned back toward me. "You know, I made Jordan an offer when she became a fashion expert like you are now. I traded her nails for a belly button piercing. What do you say? Are you willing to make the same trade?"

I looked down at my nails. They needed a lot of work. I vaguely remembered biting them when I was thinking through a coding problem. The problem with Dr. Diamond's offer was belly button piercings had gone out of style. Most women who had them done had taken them out and allowed them to close up.

I closed my eyes, trying to think. Suddenly an image of me tending an outdoor cooktop wearing nothing but an apron while a faceless man came up behind me and started to fuck me. Deep down, I knew that image should have frightened me, or at the very least disgusted me. However, I couldn't help but look on that scene and get wet from it.

The apron barely covered my nipples, leaving large amounts of side boob visible. The short apron did little to cover my legs, only just covering my pussy from the front. However, I wore nothing else, giving the man in the image unfettered access to me from behind.

I moaned as I imagined a big hard cock filling me from behind. Even now, fully dressed, I could almost convince myself that the image inside my head was real.

"Don't make me burn it," I said in my head, referring to the gumbo I had cooking on the cooktop. I had never been one to do much cooking. I fully expected, once my tech company went public, that I would use my new-found wealth to hire all the help I would need, including a personal cook.

Now, however, I could not imagine doing such a thing. My place was in the kitchen, cooking for my man, whoever that man was. My place was to stay home and tend to the house, cleaning and cooking. On weekends, we could go hiking, with me wearing as little clothing as I could get away with, enticing my man to fuck me out in the hills or the forest or wherever we found ourselves. He could fuck me any way he wanted. My body was like his plaything. No kink was too much.

"Like, holy shit," I cried out as I realized the extent of the changes to my mind.

Dr. Diamond simply smirked. "So what do you say to my offer? You get the piercing and I'll make sure your hair, makeup, and nails are perfect for when you go back on stage."

Fashion was much more than about clothes. And Dr. Diamond had just listed off the trinity of things I now cared about. I couldn't control my clothes. That was up to the show. But I could control the rest. And all I had to do was get a piercing that would be easy to hide and might come back into fashion eventually. If not, I could always take it out and let the hole close up after the show ended.

"Like, totally do it," I finally said. The trade was well worth it with my new hobbies.

The wardrobe man came in, followed by another man. They sat me back down in the chair and started in on my makeover. Meanwhile, Dr. Diamond focused on my belly-button. Apparently he had a machine that could give me the piercings and make it heal in record time, all without any pain.

"Oh god," I cried out as the work on my hair and face were nearly finished. The application of pink lipstick on my lips at the same time that my hair was getting brushed sent me over the edge. "Yes, yes, yes."

My eyes rolled up into the back of my head, my vision turned white and I dug my new long pink colored nails into the arm rests of the chair as I finally reached orgasm. It was pure relief rushing through my body, the release of all that pent up energy sending me over the edge.

"I might have overdone it a little," Dr. Diamond commented to the two men working on my hair and makeup.

"No," said one of the men as I slumped back into my chair. "I think you hit the sweet spot. Even if she wins, she will still be a bimbo."

I didn't like the sound of that, but I didn't dare argue. I finally recovered from my orgasm as everything finished up.

"There we go," Dr. Diamond said. "Alexis, you look perfect now, if I do say so myself. Come and take a look at yourself."

I took Dr. Diamond's hand as he helped me up from the chair and guided me back toward the mirror. The moment I saw myself, I was overcome with a sense of satisfaction. I looked fantastic. I looked better than I ever had before. I looked perfect.

The pink lips and pink nails nicely contrasted with my platinum blonde hair. And wearing it down was definitely my preference. It was styled in loose waves down my back, tickling the top of my ass. It was long and would be difficult to manage, but I was fine with that. Long hair was fashionable and I intended to keep it as long as I could.

And to be honest, as out of style as a bellybutton piercing

might be, it did look good having something to highlight my taut midriff. If I was going to keep showing that much skin, I might as well have something there to draw attention to it. After all, not everyone wanted to stare at my tits or my ass all the time. I mean, sure, most people did, but there were exceptions to that.

As I stepped out onto the stage, I did so with an extra jump in my step. The burly stagehand gave my ass a slap as I walked by him. I turned and waved back to him, even blowing him a kiss before I made my way to my seat on the dais.

The crowd cheered as I expected them to, but there were more hoots and wolf whistles than ever before. And I was perfectly fine with that. I knew I was a fine looking woman. Yes, I looked like a bimbo. I talked like one too. But there were certain things I needed to embrace and being the center of attention for my style and appearance was at the top of the list.

"Wow," Philbert said when I sat down across from him and the cheers from the audience died down. "Alexis, you look fantastic."

"Like, thanks," I said, before blowing Philbert a kiss of his own. That seemed to work as a stand-in for licking my lips. I didn't want to ruin my lipstick. I didn't have more to apply until I returned backstage.

"Obviously your sense of fashion had changed," Philbert said as he looked me up and down. "But what else has changed for you?"

"Um," I said, as I tried to collect my thoughts. My backstage orgasm had been a big help, but I could already feel my arousal growing again. The walk out onto the stage had not helped matters, nor had the way my hair bounced and swished with each step I took. "I think I'm, like, a super good cook now. I'll have to, you know, see when I get home and stuff. And, I'm basically open to, like, everything when it comes to sex. No kink is, like, too strange."

"What about Anything Outdoors?" Philbert asked. "We haven't had anyone get that before."

"The fun doesn't, like, need to stay in the bedroom," I said with a giggle and a wink.

The crowd went wild for that. They all knew what I was talking about. Of course, the whole problem with being so much more sexually open was the fact I didn't have a steady partner. I didn't have anyone who I would normally consider being intimate with. However, I didn't want to be labeled a slut either. I was going to need to find a man when this was all over, whether I won or lost.

"That certainly sounds like fun," Philbert said, trying not to smile too widely. I noticed how he shifted in his seat. I had little doubt he was trying to hide an erection. Just looking at my body was enough to get my juices flowing. I could only guess how hard it would be for a man, even one as experienced with bimbos as Philbert was.

"It, like, totally is," I said, filling the space. It seemed my mouth simply moved on its own at times, agreeing with whatever was said. That didn't bode well for me in the future, making me a bit of a pushover, but it was something I was going to have to live with.

"You're back after a major trip backstage," Philbert said. "You've had four new hobbies added to your mind. You currently stand at $10,000 on the Money Board, but on the seventh rung of the Bimbo Board. You are two wrong answers away from becoming a complete bimbo, but you are five right answers away from becoming the first ever winner on Truth or Bimbo, College Edition or not."

Philbert tried to make it sound like I had a chance. I appreciated that. Now that I had won $10,000, there was a part of me that wanted to walk away. I could do that and I'd figure something out about funding my tech company. But walking away felt wrong. I felt the need to keep playing. There was still hope. And it was that hope that I was going to cling to.

"So the question I have to put to you, Alexis," Philbert said, "is whether you want to keep playing Truth or Bimbo College Edition?"

I required no time to think of my answer. There was still a sparkle of hope. I could still win this thing. And maybe I could use some of the winnings to turn me back to some semblance of my former self. Although the body could stay, with a few small tweaks. But the mind stuff needed to change. Actually, keeping my fashion sense would be nice. So too would be my home ec knowledge. And actually, I wouldn't mind keeping the interest in the various kinks and the outdoors. So it was just my speech that I wanted to change back. That wasn't a big deal.

"Let's, like, totally do this," I said excitedly.

16

"All right, Alexis," Philbert said. "Let's get rolling soon on your next question. Are you ready?"

"I'm, like, super ready, Philbert," I said. "You should, like, totally ask away."

Philbert chuckled before his expression turned serious. "Very well. Here we go. Among land animals, what species have the largest eyes? Is it the African elephant, the buffalo, the mountain gorilla, or the ostrich?"

Deep down, I had been hoping for another computer question. After all, that was what I was best at. But shouldn't have gotten my hopes up. The producers had probably finished those off. It was just going to be these random hard questions the rest of the way. Bimbo here I come, I guess.

"That's, like, really hard," I said before I started to giggle. My mind filled with the image of a cock. It was a hard cock.

I shook my head, trying to clear it, only to have my hair rub against the back of my seat, sending a shiver down my spine.

"Yes, I can imagine some people might find it hard,"

Philbert said stoically. "But that doesn't help you answer the question."

"You're, like, totally right," I said.

I tried to clear my mind of everything but the question at hand. Which of those animals had the biggest eyes? It had to be a big animal, I was sure of it.

"Ostrich doesn't, like, make sense," I thought out loud. "It's too small. And I don't, like, know how big a mountain gorilla really is, but it's not super big, I don't think, you know?"

"I can see where your train of thought is taking you," Philbert said encouragingly.

"Like, yeah," I said. "And, like, the African elephant is totally the biggest animal, so I'm going to choose that."

"You've decided on the African elephant?" Philbert asked.

The truth was, I really didn't know, but I was pretty sure elephants were the biggest animals on land and so it was bigger than the other three listed. As the biggest, it would make sense to have the biggest eyes.

"Like, totally," I said. "I choose the elephant."

"I must say," Philbert said. "That was very fast. Hopefully all of your new hobbies, especially the Anything Outdoors category, has made you smarter about animal biology."

I didn't like Philbert's remark about my hobbies making me more knowledgeable. The truth was, I was only guessing. But it seemed logical that the largest animal would have the biggest eyes. Now I just had to cross my fingers that I had been right.

The suspenseful music played and the lights flashed. I could feel my heart pounding in my chest. I had to be right. If I lost, it would mean I was only one wrong answer away from losing my IQ and becoming a complete bimbo. I wouldn't just look and talk like a bimbo. I would be a bimbo through and through.

"The land animal with the largest eyes is…" Philbert said once the music stopped. This time he did pause for greater effect. "The ostrich."

"Like, wait," I said, completely shocked. "That totally can't be, like, right."

"I assure you," Philbert said calmly. "The ostrich has the largest eyes."

I crossed my arms underneath my tits and pouted. This game was losing its fun. I kept losing. Then again, maybe I wasn't as smart as I thought I was. I knew there were gaps in my knowledge base. I spent too much time with my eyes staring at a computer monitor for me to have a sense of these things. I hadn't even been to a zoo since I was a little girl.

"While Alexis comes to terms with her wrong answer," Philbert continued, "let us talk about the next category on the Bimbo Board. She has now reached Mood. This new mood of Alexis' will create a baseline for her. It will be her natural state unless another mood overrides it."

I could remember back to that first show. Jordan was given Joyful. When she returned, it was like she was an entirely different person. She was happy about everything. Almost nothing could get her down, even when she lost the last question, she still smiled about it.

"And the options are," Philbert announced, "Flirty, Bitchy, Lustful, and Joyful."

Joyful remained a popular choice, but I had seen all four of them at various points over the past year. Bitchy was especially interesting, since it always seemed to give the contestant a superior view of themselves. That was made even funnier when they lost their intelligence.

"Any thoughts on your new personality?" Philbert asked.

I sat there, thoughtful for a moment, trying to collect my thoughts. I was finding it hard to concentrate, what with my body screaming at me, begging for sexual attention and my new desire to always be fashionable. I was spending too many brain cells trying to look the best I could, almost posing on my seat.

Maybe that was why I missed the last question and didn't see the elephant for what it was, bait to go down the wrong path. My mind was getting torn in too many directions. There was my need for sex. There was my need to look good. And There was my need to plan out what I was going to cook for dinner for the next week. That was all fighting against the task immediately in front of me.

"I've, like, totally seen them all before," I finally said. "I don't really like Bitchy though, you know?"

Philbert nodded his head in agreement. "That is an interesting one. But it's not up to either of us. And this time it's not up to our studio audience either. It's up to your benefactor, Alexis. Is there anything you want to say to him before he calls?"

"Um," I said, beginning to think. "Just, like, be nice, you know?" I followed my statement, which turned into a question of its own, with a giggle. I sounded like a complete moron, but I couldn't help that. The truth was, it was all out of my hands.

Philbert chuckled. "I think I know what you mean."

Philbert's phone rang a moment later. He picked it up and put it to his ear. Now all I could do was wait to find out my fate.

17

As Philbert returned his phone to his pocket, he smiled. I tried to return the smile. I wanted to look happy about my circumstances. I kept talking myself into the idea that there was hope for me. I kept finding ways to keep playing, even when the odds were clearly stacked against me. And those odds kept getting worse and worse, yet I continued to play on.

"Alexis, your benefactor has come to a conclusion," Philbert said. "He wishes you to be Flirty."

And just like that, I knew where my future would lie. I would forever more by the hot girl who flirted with everyone. I wouldn't necessarily make overt overtures. I wouldn't say I wanted to fuck someone outright, but I would certainly hint at my desire.

There went my chance to avoid being called a slut. Looking like I did, talking like I did, and now adding a specific way of acting, that was my future. I would forever more be a shameless flirt. That was to be my life.

"What do you think of your benefactor's choice, Alexis?" Philbert asked.

I hung my head. "I guess I was, like, hoping for Joyful," I said sullenly.

"I wouldn't worry too much about it," Philbert said. "After your short trip backstage, you won't even know to think differently."

I know Philbert was trying to help, but it wasn't enough to change my mind. Not that any of the options were ideal. They all would have left me significantly changed.

"I'm sorry you feel down," Philbert said. "But it is time to send you backstage." He turned to the audience. "When Alexis returns, we will see a whole new version of her. And I'm certain she will enjoy herself."

The audience cheered as I made my way off the stage. I tried to smile and wave, but I just didn't have it in me anymore. I felt completely defeated. This was the end of me, I was certain of it.

"Ah, my favorite soon to be bimbo returns," Dr. Diamond said.

I ignored him as I shuffled over to the chair and threw myself down into it. I landed with a thud, but I didn't care. Dr. Diamond approached me carefully. He bent down in front of my sullen face and tried to get me to react. But I looked right through him. I didn't even react by licking my lips or making some other action.

"Hmm, well that's no fun," Dr. Diamond said.

If I thought he might leave me alone and stop the game, I would have been very mistaken. Dr. Diamond seemed to have no qualms about sticking the helmet on my head, careful not to disturb my hair style.

My vision went dark, all light cut off from my eyes. But that only lasted a moment. Before I knew it, the lights began to flash. I didn't even bother to close my eyes. It wouldn't matter. I was powerless against Dr. Diamond.

When the lights stopped, it was only another moment

before the lights of the room returned to me. I looked up into Dr. Diamond's face and smiled.

I didn't know why I smiled. I knew I had been depressed only a few minutes before, but sadness was no longer an emotion I felt capable of feeling. There was only joy and a desire for flirty fun.

"How do you feel?" Dr. Diamond asked.

"I, um, like, feel super good," I said, smiling up at the man who had recreated me. "You've been , like, super nice to me, and I was being, like, a total bitch, you know?"

"Oh, I know," Dr. Diamond said.

"So I was, like, wondering how to make it up to you."

Even as I sat there, I reached out with a long-nailed hand and gently ran my fingertips down Dr. Diamond's exposed forearm.

Dr. Diamond looked uncomfortable.

"I wish I could help you," he said, "but I'm not allowed until after the show."

"Are you, like, totally sure?" I asked as I gracefully rose to my feet.

I ran a hand across Dr. Diamond's chest. I could feel strong muscles underneath his lab coat and shirt.

"Please, Dr. Diamond," I said.

"Call me Double D," he choked out.

"Like, okay, Double D," I cooed in his ear, letting my lips gently brush against his jaw.

The pleasure I received from that motion, letting them rub against his jaw line, was exquisite. I could feel my pussy growing wet. I was definitely ready to be fucked. And with Double D right there, I wanted it to be him to fuck me. He had made me what I was. I was a hot and fashionable woman who was happy and flirty.

I lost all track of time as I flirted and attempted to seduce Double D. Yet somehow he managed to stand up to my temptations. Then before I knew it, the burly stagehand was standing beside me. He held me by the arm and guided me away from Double D.

I wanted to stop and flirt with the stagehand.

"You're, like, so strong," I said, trying to get a conversation going.

However, the stagehand ignored me as he suddenly sent me shooting out onto the stage.

"And it's the new Alexis," Philbert said in greeting. It seemed like the production staff were not quite ready for my return.

I didn't mind all that though. I smiled, I waved, I blew kisses to the crowd. Everyone seemed to love me, and to be honest, I loved them too.

I ran a hand along my collarbone, trying to draw more eyes to my tits as I walked toward the dais. Once I was seated, I posed for everyone.

"Like, hi there," I said as I batted my eyelashes toward the crowd.Even though I couldn't see them underneath the bright studio lights, I could hear them and that was all that mattered.

"Welcome back, Alexis," Philbert said. "You look much happier than when you left us a little while ago."

"And, like, sexier," I said. "I'm super happy and, like, totally sexy now."

Philbert chuckled. "Yes, indeed you are. I was a little worried about you when you left, but it's good to see you smiling again."

"I, like, love to smile." I said.

The truth was, I suspected Double D did more than make me flirty. I was pretty sure he made me joyful too, probably because I was so sullen. However, as I sat before Philbert now, I didn't care about what had been done to me. I felt great. I was happy and I was sexy. Wasn't that all that really mattered? Whatever else happened to me, I was going to be fine with, happy even. The world was such a beautiful and sexy place and I had become deeply in tune with that.

"That is always good," Philbert said. "Your smile lights up the room. We probably don't need as many stage lights on with how radiant your smile is."

"You're, like, such a charmer, you know?" I said as I put my hand up like I was hiding behind it, pretending to be embarrassed about the compliment I had just been given. In reality, that compliment went straight to my head. I loved hearing it. I wanted to hear more compliments. It felt good to be desired and wanted. I wanted to feel that more and more.

Philbert chuckled. "Yes, I'm certain the wrap party tonight will be a fun one. But back to the game at hand. You've reached the fifth level of the Money Board, but you're now standing on the impressive eighth step of the Bimbo Board. The game is reaching its final stages. Alexis, are you ready to continue playing Truth or Bimbo College Edition?"

"Like, of course," I said as I started blowing kisses to a roaring audience.

18

It was amazing how much the game had changed in the previous round. I had gone from sullen and depressed to happy and definitely flirty. Despite the now terrible odds, I was still happy to keep playing. This game was fun and there was no other way I would have ever been this sexy looking without missing all those previous questions.

I was definitely coming around to the opinion that my old life hadn't been worth it, even if I had an idea that could radically disrupt the online world. That success, and the stress that came with it, could not compare to the light and fluffy feeling that seemed to permeate every square inch of my body. I simply radiated happiness. Whatever happened next, was going to be just fine by me.

"Alexis," Philbert said to get my attention. "This next question is the equivalent of a match point in tennis. If you miss this next question, you will lose the game and end up with your IQ reduced to that of a bimbo. If you answer correctly, you will delay that ending, possibly reaching the point where you win the game. I'm going to give you one last chance to back out. Do you want to keep playing."

"Like, of course I do," I said with a giggle. "Don't you want to see me as a happy, flirty, and sexy bimbo?"

"That is not up to me," Philbert said. He pulled at his shirt collar. My flirtations were getting to him. Poor man. I would have to find a way to thank him later.

"If you are ready," Philbert continued, "I will ask you the next question. What is the total number of pins in a traditional parallel port connector? Is it 5, 14, 25, or 27?"

"Ooh, like, another computer question," I said, bouncing in my seat and clapping my hands. "I'm, like, super good at those. I'm totally a computer genius person."

I knew I sounded like a complete idiot, but I didn't care. All I knew was I finally had a good chance of getting another question right. It had been ages since that last happened.

"Then there is still hope for you," Philbert said.

"So there's, like, pins for data, output control, input control, and ground," I said as I started thinking through what was in the parallel port. "But, like, how many of each?"

"That is a big part of the question," Philbert said.

I started trying to count on my fingers, but quickly ran out of fingers. Somehow I knew there were eight data pins. That also meant there were eight ground pins. That was important. And that number together, added up to more than the first two answer options of 5 and 14. That meant it had to be 25 or 27. That also meant there had to be an odd number of either input control pins or output control pins.

"So, like, the first two answers aren't big enough, you know?" I said.

"I don't know, but go ahead," Philbert countered.

I smiled at him, letting my tongue dart out and lick my lips quickly. However, that left me distracted as my arousal spiked.

"What was I, like, saying?" I said, trying to find my train of thought.

"You said the answers of 5 and 14 were too small," Philbert prompted me, helping me get back on track. After all, it had been his comment that had led to my distraction.

"Oh, yeah, that's right," I said. "I can be, like, such a dum-dum sometimes."

I knew I sounded like a bimbo, even more than I really was, but I didn't have time to worry about that. Even the audience laughed at me, but I ignored them. I needed to focus on the question at hand and find a solution. Was the answer 25 or 27?

After several moments of deep thought, it occurred to me that I did not know which it was. I might have been a computer genius by some definitions, but there were certain things I didn't know. And the truth was, parallel ports were old technology at this point. USB was the catchall technology now. Many computers didn't even have parallel ports anymore. Laptops certainly didn't.

"Based on your information about parallel ports," Philbert said, "you've narrowed your choices down to two, those being 25 pins and 27 pins. Any thoughts about how to differentiate the two?"

"I, um, like, don't know," I said. "I mean, I know computers and stuff, but I don't, like, use parallel ports. I do more, like, software stuff."

"That is problematic," Philbert said with an even tone. "So it seems like you know just enough to narrow the problem down, but not enough to actually answer it."

"Totally," I said, happily. "You, like, totally get me, you know?"

Philbert smiled, but said nothing.

With Philbert's silence, I went back to thinking about parallel ports and the number of pins the connectors had. Clearly, the number of pins was odd, since that was what I had left, odd numbers. And there wasn't much difference between 25 and 27. The difference was one input control pin and one output control pin. I just didn't know how many of those there were. Was it four and five or five and six?

Then it dawned on me. I felt like a lightbulb turned on inside my head. I was certain this was it. I didn't know how I knew, but I could just picture the answer in my head.

"I'm, like, gonna choose 27," I finally said.

Philbert looked a little taken aback at my sudden response. However, once he recovered, he began to probe, "What makes you choose 27?"

"I, like, made a picture in my head and I totally counted 27 pins," I said.

"That is impressive," Philbert responded. "You are positive the answer is 27?"

"Totally," I said. "I can see it super clearly."

"Very well," Philbert said. "But I'm going to give you one last chance to back out and switch your answer. This could be your last question if you get it wrong."

"I, like, know that," I said. "But I'm totally right about this. The answer is, like, 27."

"Alexis says the answer is 27," Philbert announced.

The suspenseful music played and the lights flashed. I didn't feel any different though. I was confident I had made the right choice. I could picture it in my mind and that was good enough for me.

"And the answer is…" Philbert said. "25 pins in a traditional parallel port. I'm sorry Alexis, but you have lost Truth or Bimbo College Edition."

"Like, what?" I said, aghast. "That's totally not right. I'm super sure the answer is, like, 27."

Philbert looked me straight in the eye, staring me down so that I couldn't even flirt with him or seduce him with my facial expressions. "No, the correct answer is 25. I'm sorry Alexis, but you lose the game."

I tried to think of another way to argue my point, but nothing came to mind. I couldn't have gotten the question wrong, could I have? It didn't make sense. I felt completely certain I had been right. There were eight data pins and eight ground pins. Then there were four output control pins and five input control pins.

"O-M-G," I said, suddenly realizing my mistake. "I'm, like, such a dummy. I totally forgot how to do math, thanking eight plus eight is, like, 18. It's totally 16."

"I tried to give you another chance," Philbert said. "However, you chose poorly. Now it's time to send you backstage for the final time. When you come back, you will be a complete bimbo."

The audience cheered as I walked off the stage. As sad as I was at losing the game, I wasn't really sad. I was happy actually. I had come on the show to win money, and I'd done that. The only problem was, I didn't win all the money I had hoped for. Still, $10,000 would be enough to buy me some new clothes. It just wouldn't be enough to jumpstart my own tech company, as I had originally planned.

And the truth was, I knew running a tech company would be beyond me. Worse, it was already beyond me. There was no way I could be an effective leader with all of my bimbo qualities, even if I had kept my smarts. I could only hope I could pass on my plans to someone else who could carry them forward.

"If it isn't Alexis," Double D said as he greeted me in his workshop.

"Like hi, Double D," I said in return. Even though he was a creep, I couldn't help but smile at him. He was kind of cute in his own way. And he was going to make me into a perfect bimbo. As sad as I should have been to lose my intelligence, I was oddly happy about it all. Without my silly brains getting in the way, I could just enjoy my life as a sexy and flirty bimbo. That seemed like a pretty nice life to me.

"Let's have you get in the chair," Double D said, directing me to sit down.

This whole action was comforting from its familiarity. I knew that my mind had been completely warped by Double D and the rules of the game show, but I was accepting of that. I didn't have it in me to fight, to be mad, or even be sad. It was like those emotions had been completely stripped out of me, removed so that I could better embrace my true nature, so I could be a better bimbo.

"Anything you want to say before I put the helmet on you?" Double D asked. He was actually being nice to me.

I smiled, but shook my head. "Just, like, do it. Turn me into a total bimbo."

"I'm glad you've come to see things my way," Double D said as he lowered the helmet on my head.

He activated it a moment later and the lights flashed before my eyes. This time I could feel it as the lights burned away at my mind. It didn't just trim back my thoughts, but wholesale chopped them off. When it was done, I could barely string more than a few sentences together.

"How do you feel?" Double D asked as soon as he pulled the helmet free from my head.

I looked up at him, licked my lips and then giggled. "I feel, um, like, super good."

Just that one short sentence, filled with filler words, left my mind feeling drained. I looked around the room and suddenly felt overwhelmed by all the machines. They were far too complicated for a bimbo like me.

"Here, let me help you up," Double D said as he took my hand and guided me to my feet.

I giggled again. "Like, thanks."

I paused for a moment, my lips moving as I tried to think,

but with no sound coming out. Double D looked at me and laughed. I didn't blame him. I was sure I looked completely silly standing there trying to think.

"You, like, totally made me into a bimbo and stuff," I finally said, realizing my struggles with thinking and speaking would be with me for the rest of my life. Not that I minded. My talents laid elsewhere. I stepped closer to Double D, placing a hand on his chest. I vaguely remembered doing this before, but not how it ended. "How can I, you know, thank you, and stuff? Is there something a bimbo like me could, you know, like, do for you?"

I could sense Double D was struggling with a decision, but I couldn't understand why. I was the bimbo here, not him. He was so much smarter than me. And all I wanted to do was make him happy.

"Alexis," Double D said, taking a step back.

"Like, call me Lexi," I countered, closing the distance on him once more.

"Lexi…"

"Time to get out there," came the call from the burly stagehand.

"Like, okay," I said, turning away from Double D and practically skipping toward the stage door. Double D was left standing there in silence. I wanted to thank him properly, but I had other places I needed to be. There was a chance I would see him later though. That would be fun.

"You're, like, really sexy with all those super big muscles," I told the stagehand at the stage door.

"We can fuck later," the stagehand said. "Now get out there."

With one big push, I flung through the door, sent out to greet all my fans.

19

I blinked several times as my eyes tried to adjust to the bright lights. The spotlights were on me as everyone cheered for me. It took me a moment to remember what I was supposed to do. Then I remembered. I needed to go see Philbert so we could talk and then end the show.

I practically skipped to my seat. My high heels didn't seem to cause me any trouble anymore.

"I'd like to introduce the new and improved Alexis," Philbert announced.

I giggled at the attention. "You should, like, call me Lexi now."

"Then let me start over," Philbert said. "I'd like to introduce the new and improved Lexi."

Again the audience cheered. I smiled and waved and blew kisses to the crowd, even though I couldn't see them with the bright lights blocking my view.

When the cheers finally died down, Philbert began to speak. "So tell me, Lexi, how do you like being a bimbo?"

"Like, it's totally great," I answered automatically. It was. I didn't need to think of an answer for that question. I loved being sexy and dumb. It was so much better than all that hard thinking and stress. I only wished I hadn't had to answer all those questions to get to this point. It would have been easier to just make me a bimbo from the beginning.

"Yes, I'm sure you feel that way," Philbert said. "And that brings our show to a close. Alexis started out as a smart and capable young woman who was clearly going places. Now she is Lexi and the only place she is going is down on the next cock she sees."

I giggled at the word cock. I also started to lick my lips, salivating. I couldn't wait to give my first bimbo blowjob. That sounded fun.

"This has been a special edition of Truth or Bimbo," Philbert continued. "I can safely say that Lexi will not be returning to Thatcher College next term. My name is Philbert Regborn and you have been watching Truth or Bimbo College Edition."

As the studio lights began to fade, I wondered aloud," Can I, like, suck cock now?" I simply couldn't get the idea of a big hard cock in my mouth out of my head.

However, before my question could be answered, the big burly stagehand was pulling me to my feet and escorting me off the stage. There was some small part of me that assumed he would take me back to the green room where I had started my night before stepping out on stage, but he instead took me to an elevator.

As soon as the elevator doors closed, I dropped to my knees, assuming that I was here to suck the stagehand's cock. I was certain he had a big one, given his huge size. But he pushed my hands away.

"Special orders," the man said. "You're not to be touched until your new owner has a chance to take you first."

My owner? That was news to me. I didn't know what he was talking about. I would have pouted over not getting to suck the stagehand's cock, but now I had a new purpose. I had an owner to please, whatever that meant.

"Come on," the stagehand said. "On your feet. I don't want anyone thinking I've spoiled you."

The more the stagehand spoke, the less sense he seemed to make. I was still getting over the fact that I had an owner. Who was he? When did he become my owner? Did he like to fuck? I wanted to fuck.

Those were all the thoughts I could muster before my brain simply stopped. My mind cleared and I just stood there, holding onto the stagehand's big arm with one hand and twirling a lock of hair in the other. The fact that twirling my hair sent shockwaves of arousal through my body didn't matter. It felt good and I enjoyed it. There was nothing more to it than that.

When the elevator doors opened, the stagehand guided me down a hallway. I had to practically run to keep up with the stagehand's long strides. My high heels forced me to take little mincing steps, which in turn made my tits bounce in my tight tank top. I smiled, finding this whole adventure to be sexy and fun. I completely forgot about the reason I was here, my mind unable to hold more than one thing in it at a time.

We finally stopped in front of a door that had the letters V, I, and P on them.

"What's, like, a V-I-P?" I asked. "Am I, like, a vip?"

The stagehand laughed openly at me. Somehow, I knew such an action should have made me sad or mad or something similar. It wasn't nice to laugh at people. But I couldn't find it in myself to be mad or sad. Instead I smiled broadly and continued twirling my hair with my fingers.

"No, you're not a VIP But your owner is."

"Ooh," I said, bouncing up onto my toes and clapping my hands in excitement. "Can I meet him?"

The stagehand didn't answer. Instead he knocked on the door.

A moment later a woman who looked as much like a bimbo as I did opened the door. She wore a tiny bikini that did little to hide her outrageous proportions. What was more, her hair looked like it was on fire whenever she moved.

"O-M-G," I practically screamed as I recognized the woman for the first time. "You're, like, Jordan, right?"

The bimbo smiled in recognition.

"Who's at the door, baby?" came a man's voice from inside the room. I couldn't see past Jordan and her sexy body.

"It's sexy Lexi," Jordan called back over her shoulder. "And she looks good enough to eat."

My pussy clenched at hearing Jordan call me sexy and good enough to eat. She was like my bimbo idol. Hearing those words about me made me feel amazing.

"Bring her in," the voice called out. "She needs to meet her new owner."

Jordan reached out a long-nailed hand and took me by the wrist. She gently pulled me into the room, leaving the burly stagehand behind. As soon as the door shut behind us, I took a moment to take in the sight before me. There were half a dozen men, along with nearly as many bimbos. One side of the room was a bank of windows looking out into the studio below. These men and the bimbos serving them were able to watch me play Truth or Bimbo down below.

Several of the men were sitting with a bimbo in their laps, some bobbing their heads on their cocks, others having their crotches sat on as hands found the bimbos' tits. All of the bimbos were dressed in little to nothing. I was the bimbo with the most clothing on in the room.

As soon as I was standing before this drop of six men, Jordan returned to one of the men. She sat down on his lap and began to pull at his tie. Just looking at her, I knew what she wanted. She wanted the man's cock and he seemed perfectly willing to give it to her.

However, there was one man who did not have a bimbo on his lap or between his legs. He sat in the middle, wearing a slim blue suit. There was a week-old beard on his chin and he had an otherwise stylish appearance. Basically, he looked like he could have come out of a magazine that focused on styles of the wealthy.

"Are you, like, my owner?" I asked as the man beckoned me to join him.

"That's the general idea," the man said. His voice sounded like honey to my ears. He sounded confident, yet kind, and forceful, but gentle.

I practically skipped to him. He stood up and caught me in his arms. He felt so strong. He wasn't necessarily as strong at the burly stagehand, but he was both physically strong and mentally commanding. He had a presence that did not rely on pure muscle. And because of that I found myself melting into his arms, letting him hold me tight as he took possession of my body, mind, and soul.

"I'm Lexi," I said as I buried my face into his chest.

"My name is Kevin," he said. "And you are going to be my sexy Lexi."

"Yes, sir," I said.

I vaguely remembered this man from my past. He was rich, having founded his own tech company like I had planned to do. He had billions of dollars to his name, both in stock and in cash. Now he spent his time investing in new companies and using his money for various philanthropic causes.

"I was your benefactor," Kevin said as he pulled me away from him and held me by the shoulders at arm's length. "Now let me get an idea of what my money bought me."

I licked my lips as I looked into Kevin's eyes. I couldn't wait for him to take me, for him to claim me, for him to stamp me as his bimbo. In that moment, I knew Kevin to be my owner and I would do everything I could to serve him.

"Yes, I definitely approve," Kevin said, assessing me.

He turned back toward the other men in the room, surveying them.

"Gentleman," Kevin began. "I think I need to get acquainted with Lexi in a more private setting. If you'll excuse me."

Before I knew what was happening, Kevin was guiding me into an adjacent room. It took me a moment before I understood what I was looking at. There was a bed and several lounge chairs. The previous room had been meant as a place to watch the show. This room was a place meant for one thing, fucking.

I would have been ready to strip off my clothes right there, but Kevin wanted to take it slow. He took his time pulling at my top, lifting up and exposing more of my taut midriff.

I reached up to start unbuttoning Kevin's shirt, but he pushed my hands away.

"You just stand there and look pretty," he said.

Luckily, that was easy for a sexy bimbo like me. Kevin ran his hands across my bare skin, teasing me with gentle caresses as his fingertips danced across my body. I shuddered in pleasure as a low moan escaped my lips.

"Yes, I like that response," Kevin said. "You're so sensitive. Every touch makes you wet."

I didn't say anything. I didn't need to say anything. He was not making wishes. He was stating facts. He was right. He was smart. And now he owned me.

When Kevin pulled my top up over my tits, I held my arms up so he could smoothly glide the top up and over my head. Still, he took his time, taking a moment to run his fingers over my tits, even pinching my already diamond-hard nipples. A louder and more desperate moan escaped my lips this time.

Once my tank top was tossed aside, Kevin turned his attention to my shorts. They were spandex and tight, doing little to hide the fact I wasn't wearing underwear. In fact, it was clearly obvious for anyone who cared to look, given the clear camel toe I sported between my legs as my fleshy pussy was held tight by the thin fabric covering it.

As Kevin turned his attention downward, so did I. But I was not concerned with my shorts. Instead, I was solely focused on the large tenting of Kevin's slacks. He was hard and, from what I could tell, he was big. He was really big.

As much as I wanted to reach out and free Kevin's cock, I held my hands to my side, knowing Kevin wanted to take his time and take the lead. I was more than happy to let him, knowing he was my dominant owner and I was his subservient bimbo. He was to lead and I was to follow. That was the natural order for a bimbo like me with a strong man like Kevin.

I barely noticed that Kevin had pulled my shorts down, except that I felt a sudden draft as cool air reached my wet and waiting pussy lips for the first time since I changed clothes on the show. That felt like a lifetime ago, occurring before I had my mind nearly wiped clean.

I stepped out of the shorts, but kept my heels on. Kevin made no move to remove my heels. He did, however, guide me toward the bed where he laid me down on my back.

I stretched and posed, cat-like as Kevin began to remove his clothes. His eyes never left me, drinking in my sexiness and my bimbo essence.

Time lost all meaning as I laid there, waiting. It could have been hours or even days as easily as it could have been mere minutes. What mattered was the connection I felt deep inside to the man who stood above me.

"Please," I begged. "Like, fuck me."

I didn't have long to wait. As soon as Kevin revealed his own taut and toned body, as well as his monster cock, he was upon me. His cock sat near my entrance, holding back just far enough to tease me.

"Sir," I said. "Your bimbo totally needs a super hard fuck."

Kevin looked me in the eyes. I saw a fire I had never seen before in a man. He looked almost possessed. It was pure passion bubbling up to the surface. It was a passion only my body could relieve him of.

I screamed out in pleasure as Kevin entered me. His cock was big, splitting me open, pushing himself into my channel with force, but going agonizingly slow. He pushed in inch by inch, until his entire cock was inside of me.

I held him tight, my long nails almost scratching his back as I gripped him, wanting to feel him inside of me forever. I had never felt this full. I had never felt this fulfilled. But now I understood my purpose. This was what I was meant for. I was just a sexy bimbo who was made for fucking by her owner.

Kevin eventually set up a steady rhythm as he sawed back and forth, thrusting in and out of me. The pleasure soon became completely overwhelming, sending me higher and higher as I climbed toward my climax.

As Kevin continued, his rhythm grew more and more urgent as he pistoned in and out of me with greater speed and force. All of my senses became focused on my pussy. That was all that mattered. It was all my brain could handle in that moment.

Somehow I knew Kevin was about to cum. He didn't announce it. He didn't need to. I was his bimbo and he could cum in me, on me, or wherever else he wanted to without telling me. And yet, I still knew, using some new sense that had been opened up to me with my bimbofication.

It was only a moment later when Kevin pushed into me one last time, driving himself as deep as he could muster, his cock sending forth a torrent of how white cum filling my needy pussy. I came with him, finally reaching the summit of my climax, my whole body pulsing with radiant orgasmic energy. My entire body sung with cascades of overwhelming pleasure as we came together.

"That was impressive," Kevin said as he withdrew his softening cock.

I immediately jumped into action, diving between Kevin's legs and began to suckle at his cock, making sure I had gotten every drop of cum from him, as well as to clean him of our combined juices. It wouldn't do to let him put his cock away soiled as it had been.

"And even more impressive," Kevin said as he watched me work without prompting. I was operating on instinct. That was most of what I had left at this point. I was too dumb to think rationally. Most of my actions were simple instincts, nothing more. What few brain cells I still had operating were focused elsewhere, anyway, namely in looking and acting as sexy as possible.

When finally I was finished cleaning Kevin's cock, I sat back and posed for my owner. I had no idea what he had planned for me. It wasn't my place to question him on such matters. As long as he kept me in sexy clothes and fucked me regularly, in any of my available holes, I would be happy.

"Damn," Kevin finally said. "I know I could have jumped in and made my offer before, but I'm glad I waited for you."

That was all I could stand. I jumped into Kevin's arms and held him tight. I fought tears of joy, not wanting to ruin my makeup. I was so happy that he had chosen me and made me his bimbo. I knew what the other Truth or Bimbo bimbos did. They did Strip Trivia nights around the country. But that wasn't for me. I wasn't a bimbo who would get used by whoever was available. I was the kind of bimbo who needed an owner, someone to take care of me as I did my best to care for their needs as well. I could not have been happier with the results of my time on Truth or Bimbo College Edition

EPILOGUE

Lexi enjoyed every moment she got to spend with Kevin. Having already made his millions, he needed little else to keep him happy. However, Lexi found herself a regular part of his life.

When Lexi first joined Kevin in his mansion overlooking the Pacific Ocean, she had no idea all that Kevin had done to close out her old life. For her, she simply moved straight into her new bimbo life, not bothering to think about her old life for a single moment.

Kevin, however, took a different view of things. He pulled her out of college. There was no way she could continue now. The IQ drop performed by Dr. Diamond had been too severe for her to ever return to academia. Kevin honestly wondered if Lexi could have completed middle school given her new outlook on life.

However, Kevin got more than a personal bimbo from his deal with Lexi. He also got access to all of her previous programming projects, including the new software platform she had been raising money for.

Kevin had been surprised when he first saw it. The software was so simple. Yet as he dived deeper into it, he saw it for what it was. The potential was off the charts. And he knew just how to implement it.

It was still a year before Kevin and his new company launched the software platform for the general public. Funding the company himself, named K&L Enterprises, he could have complete control.

When Kevin walked into the debut party, everyone cheered for him. All of his employees understood what they were working on and the potential it would have to supplant the tech giants, providing something both good and secure.

However, this was more than just a party. It was a chance to show off Lexi, now his fiancée, to the world. They had already seen her descent into bimbodom, but now they could see her as the trophy wife she was about to become.

For Lexi's part, she had spent all day getting ready. First she needed to get her hair and nails done, along with professional grade makeup. These were things she regularly partook in, with Kevin always footing the bill. But she knew this night was special, so she pulled out all the stops, making sure everything about her was perfect.

Her outfit for the night was simple. It was a short and low-cut pink dress paired with sky-high pink heels. However, the dress showed far more of her body than was generally considered appropriate, but that was mostly Kevin's idea.

He liked her to wear revealing clothes that sometimes bordered on the trashy. That was why he had her get a tongue piercing. It wasn't the sort of thing a classy woman would get, but he liked it on her and he loved the way it felt when she sucked his cock.

As Kevin and Lexi walked into the party, she was still enjoying the taste of Kevin's cum as she had spent the drive to the party on her knees in the limo, sucking Kevin's cock. Not that anyone at the party knew any of that.

Instead, what they saw was Kevin walk in wearing his signature blue suit and Lexi wearing a pink dress that made it impossible not to think about her tits. Not only was the dress low-cut, but there was a large cutout at her sternum that effectively made it so her tits were only covered by a narrow band of cloth, tied together in the middle.

Lexi was happy to acquiesce to Kevin's preferences. The pink plastic hoop earrings and bright pink lipstick further highlighted the kind of woman she was. She was a bimbo and she was never happier than when she was on Kevin's arm in public.

Well, maybe that was not entirely true. It was he sex that made her happiest. Anywhere, anytime, Lexi was ready for him.

The entire night, Lexi never left Kevin's side. She laughed at all of his jokes, she giggled whenever someone tried to ask her a question, and she managed to drag Kevin off for a few quiet moments so she could serve him on her knees before Kevin gave the official toast that launched his latest venture, something that never would have been possible unless Lexi had come into his life.

Lexi was the happiest she had ever been, finding a life of serving better than one of school and business. She was happy with her new life as a trophy wife and she was proud to have created the foundations that led to her husband's further success. If she had the chance to do it all over again, she wouldn't want to change a thing.

Sadie Thatcher is a longtime author of erotic fiction, especially related to transformations and bimbofication. She likes to say "I have thrown off the shackles of my conservative upbringing and now write erotic stories."

She maintains several blogs devoted to her writings, including a behind the scenes look at her writing process, and bimbos in general, as well as highlights works by other authors. They can be found at:

https://authorsadiethatcher.tumblr.com
https://buildingbettergiggles.tumblr.com

Subliminal Society

Inheritance

Company Morale

His Bimbo Girlfriend

The Curse of Playing Bimbo Tag

The Curse of Playing Bimbo Tag: Jenna or Jenni

The Bimbo Professor: The Curse of Playing Bimbo Tag Book 3

Anything for the Job

Anything for the Job 2

Anything for His Job

The Bimbo in the Mirror

The Bimbo in the Mirror 2

Bimbo Halloween

Bimbo Christmas

Dorm Room Bimbo

Carissa's Magic Pen

Spirit Walk

Muscle Memory

The Case of the Bimbo Wife

Changes

New Year New You

The Bimbo Dream

The Wedding Gift

The Cure

Backfire

Workout Buddies

Bim & Bo Yoga

Wishing for Each Other

Bimbo Roots

Body Swap Rings: Happy Anniversary

Body Swap Rings 2: Wedding Night

The Bimbo Experience

The Bimbo Experience 2

The Bimbo Experience 3some

The 4th Bimbo Experience

Bimbo Genes

Bimbo Genes II: The Virus

The Bimbo Genes III: The Epidemic

Bimbo Juice: Blue Raspberry

Bimbo Juice: Grape

Bimbo Juice: Mango

Bimbo Juice: Pineapple

Bimbo Juice: Red Apple

Bimbo Juice: Veggie

Bimbo Juice Gone Wild: The Muse

Bimbo Juice Gone Wild: Street Racer

Bimbo Juice Gone Wild: Score